ALSO BY KARIN TIDBECK

Amatka

Jagannath

THE MEMORY THEATER

THE

MEMORY
THEATER

Karin Tidbeck

PANTHEON BOOKS

NEW YORK

Library of Congress Cataloging-in-Publication Data
Name: Tidbeck, Karin, [date] author.
Title: The memory theater / Karin Tidbeck.
Description: First edition. New York : Pantheon Books, 2021
Identifiers: LCCN 2020021201 (print). LCCN 2020021202 (ebook).
ISBN 9781524748333 (hardcover). ISBN 9781524748340 (ebook).
Subjects: GSAFD: Fantasy fiction.
Classification: LCC PT9877.3.145 M46 2021 (print) |
LCC PT9877.3.145 (ebook) | DDC 839.73/8—dc23
LC record available at lccn.loc.gov/2020021201
LC ebook record available at lccn.loc.gov/2020021202

www.pantheonbooks.com

Jacket background image: Mystic, 2004 (detail) by
Magdolna Ban. © Magdolna Ban/Bridgeman Images
Jacket design by Kelly Blair

Manufactured in Canada
First Edition

2 4 6 8 9 7 5 3 1

To my grandmother Greta,
who came down from the mountain

PART I

THE GARDENS

Dora and Thistle spent the party hiding under a side table. The lords and ladies twirled between the marble statues on the dance floor, heels clattering on the cracked cobblestones to a rhythm that slid back and forth in uneven and hypnotic syncopation. One-two-three-four-five, one-two-three-four-five-six. Satin skirts brushed against brocade coats; playful eyes glittered in powdered faces. Lady Mnemosyne, resplendent in her laurel wreath and leafy dress, watched from her throne. It was like any other feast in this place, in eternal twilight, under a summer sky. At the edge of the dance floor, servants waited by buffet tables laden with cornucopias and drink.

Thistle sighed. "You've got grass all over your front."

Dora blinked and peered down at her pinafore. It did have grass on it. The dress itself smelled sour and sat too tight over her chest and upper back, and the edges of the veil around her shoulders were frayed. She was not at all as clean and neat as Thistle, who sat with the coattails of his celadon livery neatly folded in his lap. His lips and cheeks were rouged, his hazel eyes rimmed with black, his cropped auburn curls slicked against his skull.

Dora reached out and rubbed the collar of Thistle's coat between her fingers. The velvet felt like mouse fur. Thistle gently pried her hand off.

"You need to be more careful," he said.

A loud crash made them jump, and Dora lifted the tablecloth to peek outside. One of the ladies had upended a buffet table and sprawled in the ruins of a cornucopia. She laughed and smeared fruit over her skirts. Thistle took Dora's free hand and began to clean her nails with a small rosewood stick.

"Servants!"

Heels clicked over the stones. A hoarse voice called out: "Servants! Servants!"

It was Lady Augusta, Thistle's mistress. Dora dropped the tablecloth. Thistle quickly veiled Dora's face and crawled away to find his lady. A shock of lily of the valley perfume stung Dora's nose, and she tried to stifle a sneeze. There was a rustle and Thistle returned and settled down next to her. He folded the veil back again.

"It's nothing. Nothing you have to worry about. Here, dry your nose."

Thistle smiled at Dora and gave her a handkerchief. His face was pale under the rouge. He continued Dora's manicure, and she gnawed on the cuticles of her other hand. Somewhere above them, Lady Mnemosyne's voice boomed in the air: "Drink to eternal beauty, my friends! Revel in our glory. Now dance and kiss and be joyful!"

Dora let the noise of applause and shouts wash over her and

relaxed into the good little pain of Thistle digging for dirt under her nails.

When she opened her eyes again, it was quiet.

"They've gone to sleep," Thistle said. "We can go."

They crawled out from under the table and picked their way across cobblestones littered with cups and crystal shards.

Thistle led Dora in an arc around the debris to where the dance floor ended and the path through the birch grove began. The black soil swallowed the sound of their footsteps, and Thistle let out a long breath. Dora took his hand as they walked between the trees in silence.

In the middle of the grove, Porla was asleep in her pool. She floated just under the surface, blond hair waving in the water like seaweed. Her greenish face looked innocent: you'd never know that her teeth were sharp and she kept the body of a dead servant under the roots of a tree that grew next to the water. She had been a lady; then she dived into the water and never left. She had tried to lure Dora and Thistle in for "tea" more than once. They gave the pool a wide berth.

A breeze wafted into the grove, thick with the smell of apples. Dora and Thistle stepped out from between the birch trees and into the orchard under the big ultramarine bowl of sky. The air bit into Dora's lungs.

The orchard's gnarled apple trees were planted in neat rows. You could stand in any spot and stretch out your arms and pretend that the trees streamed from your fingertips. The branches hung heavy with fruit: every other tree carried big red apples, and the rest juicy-looking green ones. Dora had compared most of the trees. They all looked the same, down to the smallest twig and fruit. The apples tasted the same, too: hard and tongue-shriveling sour for the green, mealy and sweet for the red. Dora sniffed an apple on the nearest tree, then bit into it. It smelled better than it tasted. Her feet made a swishing noise in the damp grass. Next to her, Thistle was quiet. She glanced at him. His steps were so light; he moved like a wading bird, like the lords and ladies. He looked so frail next to her, little stolen boy. Dora should be minding him instead of the other way around. She didn't say this out loud, just stopped and held him close.

"What are you doing?" Thistle mumbled against her shoulder.

He had stopped speaking in the boy voice now that they were alone. Male servants with low voices were doomed. The lords and ladies hadn't noticed because Thistle was short and good at shaving.

"You're so small."

He chuckled. "I can't breathe."

Dora let go again. Thistle looked up at her and smiled. The paint around his eyes was smudged.

"Come on, sister." He took her hand.

At the edge of the orchard, the conservatory's great cupola loomed against the wall of forest that surrounded the Gardens. It was the biggest structure in the realm, a complicated wooden lattice inlaid with glass panes that reflected the hues in the evening sky. In the conservatory, little orange trees stood in a circle around three divans, lit by flickering wax candles. Here rested the enormous Aunts, attended by their Nieces. The Aunts ate and ate until they could grow no bigger. Then they died, and their Nieces cut them open to reveal a new little Aunt nestled around the old Aunt's heart. The old body was taken away to make food for the new little Aunt, who grew and grew, until she was done and the cycle repeated itself.

The lords and ladies didn't come here. Neither did the other servants, who said that the Aunts were too strange. Whenever their masters slept, as they did between parties, this was a good place for Dora and Thistle to sit in peace. One of the apple trees grew close to the dome's side, and that was where Dora had made a secret place: a little nest made of discarded pillows and blankets in the hollow between the tree and the wall.

Thistle sat down and leaned back against the tree trunk. Dora lay down next to him and rested her head in his lap. She took one of his hands and slid her fingers up inside his sleeve where the skin was warm. The ornate scars on his skin felt silky under her fingertips. Thistle flinched a little, then relaxed again.

"I saw something," he said. "When Lady Augusta called for me."

"Oh." After a moment, Dora realized she should probably ask, "What did you see?"

Thistle shook his head. "I'm not sure."

Dora waited. Thistle took so long that when he spoke again, she had stopped listening and had to ask him to repeat himself.

"My mistress looked at me and said, 'How are you alive?'" Thistle said.

His hand gripped Dora's hair so hard it hurt.

"Ow," Dora said.

Thistle didn't seem to notice.

"She's going to do something to me," he said. "Or she thinks she's done something. She might try it again."

The lords and ladies didn't move through time like others did. They lived through the same evening, over and over again. They rose from their beds, threw a party or organized a game, and reveled through the twilight until they fell asleep. Then they awoke from their stupor, and the party began anew. Their minds worked in loops; they would forget what they had done and remember things they hadn't done yet.

Their servants, however, were children who had wandered into the surrounding forest from the outside, lured in by fairy lights and the noise of revels. The lords and ladies stole the children's names, marking and binding each child to its new master, taking all but the faintest memories of their former lives away. But the children weren't touched by the same ageless magic that surrounded their masters. They grew up, and the patterns that were carved into them became complete. When that happened, they were killed for sport and eaten.

"If I just had my true name back," Thistle said, "I would be free from Augusta. We could run away from here before anything happens. And with my name I would remember where I came from and find a way back to my parents. You could live with us."

"You've looked for your name everywhere," Dora said. "You said it's not written down, it's not caught in a jar, it isn't embroidered on a handkerchief."

Thistle hung his head.

Dora pried Thistle's fingers loose from where they were stroking her hair. "I won't let her hurt you. Now tell my story."

Thistle let out a shaky laugh. "How many times do you need to hear it?"

Dora smiled. "I like hearing it."

"All right," Thistle said. "Once upon a time there was a lonely lord called Walpurgis. He was rich and beautiful and comfortable, but he wanted a child. In this land, however, no one had children, for they had become timeless and forgotten how to make them.

" 'Oh, how I wish I had a child of my own,' Lord Walpurgis

would say, and put his head in his hands. 'Someone who was part of me.'

"So it came to pass that a visitor arrived, a traveler who called herself Ghorbi, and she came from far away.

"Walpurgis sought her out, and said, 'My good woman, will you help me? For I would like a child of my own.'

" 'I will help you,' Ghorbi replied, 'but you must know this: if you mistreat her, she will not be yours.'

"Still, Walpurgis insisted, and he paid Ghorbi in precious stones. She took a bottle of his seed and went away. Then she returned, and she wasn't alone.

" 'Walpurgis, I have your daughter,' Ghorbi said. 'This is Dora.'

"She stepped aside, and lo! There was a girl. She was as tall as Walpurgis, her shoulders broad and strong, her eyes dark as the earth, and her hair like white feathers.

" 'Father,' said the girl, and her voice was like the blackbird's song.

" 'She was grown from your seed in the earth,' Ghorbi said. 'She is half of the mountain, and half of you.'

"But Walpurgis hesitated. 'I thank you for this gift,' he said. 'But this creature is too precious. I am not worthy.'

" 'A bargain's a bargain,' Ghorbi replied. 'I have delivered what you asked for.'

"And then she was gone.

"Walpurgis had a good heart, but even though he tried, he couldn't take care of Dora. He was simply not very good at being a parent, since he couldn't recall ever being a child. The court was angry with him and demoted him to chamberlain, for they had all sworn not to bear children of their own.

"Walpurgis found a friend for Dora, a boy called Thistle, who was a page to the lady Augusta.

"The lords and ladies said, 'You can take care of her better than we. Let her be veiled, lest we are reminded of our failure.'

"Thistle was happy to care for Dora. They loved each other like brother and sister."

Dora closed her eyes. Her favorite part was coming.

"Finally, after being a terrible father, Walpurgis began to understand," Thistle continued. "He finally understood what love was, and that he must take care of Dora. And so he took her back, and he saw how well Thistle had cared for her. And he promised to love her and asked her forgiveness for his neglect."

"Really?" Dora asked.

Thistle stroked her hair. "Really."

Far away, someone blew a whistle. Thistle carefully lifted Dora's head and stood up.

"There's a croquet game," he said. "I have to go."

Dora watched him walk out into the orchard, then followed at a distance.

2

Hidden behind an oak at the edge of the game lawn, Dora watched them play. She kept her veil drawn over her face. The pale lords and ladies loitered on the grass, leaning on croquet clubs and each other. Lady Mnemosyne watched from her seat on the podium, eyes shadowed under her wreath, her skirts spread out like a willow tree. Walpurgis lay on the grass at her feet, propped up on his elbow. The left half of his white coat was spattered with something sticky-looking. Next to him, the twins Cymbeline and Virgilia embraced on their divan. Cymbeline's crinoline was covered in chestnut leaves; Virgilia's dress was woven out of peacock feathers. At the edge of the lawn, Augusta's sister Euterpe was already drunk, rolling around in the grass dressed only in a thin shift. Hyssop, Virgilia's page boy, stood at attention nearby, holding a tray of drinks and sweetmeats. Like the other servants, he was good at not moving. Moving drew attention.

In the center of the lawn, surrounded by little arches stuck into the ground, the lady Augusta stared at a striped ball by her feet. She looked formidable in her brilliant blue coat and knee pants; her mahogany hair was freshly curled, her face a work of art. Thistle stood at her elbow, hands clasped behind his back, eyes wandering over the lawn. He looked into the trees and briefly met Dora's gaze. His eyes widened a fraction, and he shook his head almost imperceptibly.

Augusta swung her club. The ball flew in a high arc and hit Hyssop. He dropped his tray and clutched his arm with a groan. The crowd on the lawn burst into cheers and applause. Mnemosyne smiled and nodded from her podium. When Hyssop straightened, Virgilia got up from the divan and slapped him. She pointed at the mess. Hyssop immediately kneeled to pick it up, his left arm shaking.

Dora watched as the game progressed. She had never understood the rules, but everyone broke into applause when the players hit the servants.

Augusta swung her club with flair; Thistle had to duck several times to avoid getting smacked. He fetched drinks when asked to and mopped the sweat from Augusta's brow with a small handkerchief.

Dora almost ran out across the lawn when Lord Tempestis landed his ball in the face of Euterpe's little page, Calla, but she knew she mustn't. It would make things worse. Calla bled all over her doublet and spat something into her hand.

At cake break, they punished Hyssop for dropping the tray. Virgilia took his jacket and shirt off. Two flower stems reached up along Hyssop's shoulder blades, and more of them meandered down his arms. Each servant had their special art, carved into them with teeth and nails: hyssop, calla, vetch, foxglove, others. And thistle.

Walpurgis and Cymbeline took each of Hyssop's arms. Virgilia sank one of her long fingernails into her page's right shoulder. Dora forced herself to watch. Hyssop deserved her bearing witness, at least. She had barged in, once, to defend a page. The lords and ladies had reacted quickly. They wouldn't strike her like they would a servant; instead, they had immobilized her with their words, but not before Dora had knocked Cymbeline to the ground and made her cry. And for Dora's rebellion, they had hurt Thistle.

Eventually, Virgilia stepped back and licked at her bloodied hand. Dora lost sight of Hyssop as the other nobles crowded in to inspect Virgilia's work and mumble their appreciation.

"His pattern is done," Walpurgis announced over the murmur.

"A hunt!" Virgilia shouted. "I call for a hunt!"

"Excellent," Mnemosyne said from her throne. "We shall have a hunt when this game is complete. Come here, little Hyssop, and sit at my feet."

Hyssop shambled over to the dais and sank down on his knees. Dora could see his face now, twisted and tearful. He knew what awaited him. So did Dora. And there was nothing she could do. Hyssop was all grown up, and his flower was finished, and so he must die.

Walpurgis waved off all the servants except Thistle, who was ordered to move the hoops around. Then Walpurgis clapped his hands, and the game resumed.

Cymbeline and Virgilia gripped their club together and swung it. Their ball hit Augusta's so hard that it rolled into the woods. The others jeered. They continued the game as Augusta walked in among the trees. She walked past the spot where Dora was hiding and deeper into the woods. She was gone for a long moment.

When Augusta came back, she was carrying a small locket in one hand and her ball in the other. She paused at the edge of the trees and peered at the people on the lawn. From where Dora was crouching, she could see the sweat that scored a pink trail down Augusta's temple. Augusta flipped the locket open. She froze, staring at whatever it was she saw, and frowned.

"I know what this is," she muttered. "What is it?"

Then she closed the locket again and slipped it into a pocket on her waistcoat. She glanced briefly over her shoulder, shrugged, and returned to the lawn.

Dora walked back the way Augusta had come. It wasn't far to the dog-rose bush where a dead man lay on the ground, faceup. He looked different: his face was lined and his hair salt-and-pepper. He was old. His clothes looked strange, the black coat oddly cut. Dora had never seen anything like this before. Children had wandered into the Gardens. Never a full-grown man. How had he gotten here? Had someone let him in? Dora left the dead man as he was.

Dora had sat down by the conservatory again when Thistle came wandering between the trees.

"There you are," he said.

He sank to the ground next to her. His kohl was running.

"Hyssop is gone," he said. "They chased him into the woods and killed him."

"I know," Dora said.

"The servants are not real people to them. Just playthings."

"Maybe you could run away again," Dora said.

Thistle looked at her. "You know what happens. We walk into the forest, and walk and walk, and then we end up in the orchard again."

It was true. Dora and Thistle had tried, many times, when everyone else was asleep. It was always the same: a long walk through the woods, in a seemingly straight line, and then in not too long the conservatory rising beyond the trees. As if the path turned back on itself. As long as Thistle was still in Lady Augusta's service, as long as she kept his true name hidden from him, he could never find his way home. And because Dora was Walpurgis's child, she was stuck, too. She wasn't a servant, yet also not a lady. Just a reminder of failure and grief, free to exist but not to be a part of anything. Walpurgis renounced her every time he saw her. But perhaps not next time. Perhaps he loved her a little. Or so she hoped.

"Thistle," Dora said. "I found something."

Thistle cleared his throat. "What did you find?"

"When they knocked the lady Augusta's ball into the forest. I saw that. And Lady Augusta walked after it, and then . . ."

Someone clapped their hands: once, twice. Calla was standing a little distance from the apple tree. Her mouth was still swollen from the ball that Lord Tempestis had shot into her face. She didn't speak; she had no tongue. It had been cut out. Her mistress liked her page mute.

Calla held her hand out to Thistle.

"Please tell me later, Dora," he said. "I have to go."

Dora followed a few steps behind Calla and Thistle. As they arrived at Augusta's pavilion, Dora snuck around to the back, where she could peek between the lavender lengths of silk. A smell of musk and lily of the valley wafted out from the interior. Augusta sat by her desk, the shiny locket in her hand. Her curls were piled high on her head, strands of them tumbling down the sides of her face. Her eyes were such a light gray that they were almost translucent. She turned around when Thistle rang the little bell above the opening.

"Boy," she said in her hoarse voice, and stood up.

Thistle looked her in the eyes; his jaw was clenched. Augusta slapped him. Thistle lowered his eyes and walked over to the bed, preparing to remove his coat. He must have been expecting her to carve him. Dora had seen it before. Thistle never complained, never asked Dora to intervene. Dora wondered how much Augusta would scream if Dora did the same to her.

"No, not now," Augusta said.

Thistle turned around. Augusta tossed the locket at him. He caught it with both hands.

"You will tell me what this is," Augusta said.

Thistle frowned at the locket and opened the lid.

"It's a watch," he said. "I have seen one, maybe before . . ."

"And what is a watch?" Augusta interrupted.

"Mistress doesn't know?"

Augusta slapped him again. "Insolence."

Her nails bit into his jaw. Thistle's eyes watered. His eyes met Dora's. Dora stood up. Thistle shook his head faintly, and Dora sat down again.

"You will tell me what a watch is," Augusta repeated.

Thistle sniffled. "It measures time."

"Show me," Augusta said.

She pulled Thistle down on the bed next to her, and put her arm around him as if she were his protector, not someone who might stick her thumbs into his eyes because he looked at her in the wrong way.

Thistle pointed at the clockface. "This hand moves forward, and then the shorter one, and then the shortest. That knob winds it up to make it run."

As he spoke, Augusta shuddered and made a noise at the back of her throat.

"I know it. Somehow, I know what this is," Augusta said. "Does it measure time?" Augusta said. "Or does it just move forward and call that time?"

Thistle blinked. "Time is time," he said. "If it goes, it goes forward, from moment to moment."

Dora remembered time. She recalled crawling out of the earth into a rosy dawn. The sun, traveling across the sky to set. Shifting light and darkness. Heat and cold. But here it was always an azure summer night, an eternal sunset tinting the western sky green and gold.

Augusta twisted the little knob on the side of the locket. A ticking sound filled the air, faint and deafening all at once. The air trembled.

"Very well," Augusta said. "That is all." Her voice echoed.

Augusta let go of Thistle's shoulders. Thistle stood up. When he was almost at the door, Augusta spoke.

"This will be our little secret. Kneel."

Thistle did as he was told. Augusta picked up a long knife that lay on her vanity. She grabbed Thistle's jaw and, with her other hand, held the knife against his throat. Dora stood up, prepared to leap through the curtains.

Thistle spoke between Augusta's fingers: "Wait!"

Augusta blinked and released Thistle's jaw. "You dare?"

"My pattern isn't done," Thistle said. "You're not allowed to kill me until it is."

"I can finish it now, if you like," Augusta replied in a sweet voice. "Undress."

"You have to call a hunt, too," Thistle said. "It's the way of the lords and ladies."

"Then I shall do so, dear," Augusta said.

"But you just had one." Thistle's voice broke. "You're not finished dining on Hyssop. The lady Mnemosyne will be angry."

"Mouthy little shit. I regret taking you at all."

"You could give me my name back," Thistle said quickly, "and I would go away and be gone from here. I would never trouble you again."

"Give it back? Go away?" Augusta smiled. "There's no leaving this place, boy."

Thistle looked at the ground.

"Take that jacket off now," Augusta said. "And your shirt."

Thistle did as he was told, folding his clothing beside him. The flower stems Augusta had carved up his arms and over his chest were raised welts against his skin. Augusta bent down and trailed the sharp nails of her right hand across his chest. Thistle froze as she pressed her index finger against his left clavicle. He gasped as her nail bit into his skin.

"Almost done," Augusta whispered. "Nearly there."

She dropped her hand and straightened. "Leave me."

Thistle stood up, blood running down his chest. He rushed to gather his things and stepped outside. Dora watched as he left, then backed away before she could be noticed. If anyone caught her, Thistle's pattern would be finished for sure.

Dora began to head to the conservatory. She passed the dining tables, where some of the servants were busy cleaning up.

The food heaped on the tables was returning to its original state: moss, bark, toads. It happened at the end of a party, when the lords and ladies had left to sink back into their stupor. All but the bones sitting in the middle of the center table. They would be buried.

Walpurgis sat in a corner of the dance floor, overseeing the cleaning procedure, wine bottle in hand. He looked up at Dora as she went past. Her heart beat stronger for a second. Perhaps this would be the day the story came true and he took her back.

"Hey!" he shouted. "Your face, cretin."

Dora quickly pulled the veil over her face. She had forgotten.

Something hit her leg: the wine bottle. It didn't break but spilled its contents over Dora's feet.

"Your fault," Walpurgis mumbled. "It's all your fault."

Every time he happened to see Dora, he said the same thing, over and over again. Your fault.

"Father," Dora whispered.

"Not your father!" Walpurgis shouted. "No. Not your father. I don't care what Mnemosyne says. You're not mine."

He said that each time as if it were the first. Dora raised her veil slightly and looked at him where he sat. He was weeping.

"Then where do I go?" she said.

"I don't care," Walpurgis replied. "Don't show your face here."

Dora found Thistle under their tree. He was curled up, seemingly asleep, a blotch of blood on his shirt. Dora wrapped herself around him. He mumbled and shifted a little against her chest.

"He still says he's not my father," Dora whispered to Thistle's sleeping form. "But I will always be his daughter."

As they lay there, the lady Augusta came walking through the orchard, the pocket watch swinging from her hand. Dora stiff-ened, ready to defend Thistle if needed. But Augusta didn't seem to notice them at all. She walked up to the conservatory, rubbed a sleeve over one of the panes, and looked inside. Staring at the watch in her hand, she twisted the little knob on the side. There was that ticking noise again, and a sense of something shifting, a twitch in the air.

"Look at that," Augusta murmured.

3

Dora ruffled Thistle's hair and stood up. Thistle was dreaming now, eyes moving behind his eyelids. She looked down at him. He should be allowed to sleep for as long as he could. She walked back through the orchard, after Augusta. Augusta would finish Thistle's pattern soon. What if Dora could find his name? Maybe there was somewhere Thistle hadn't looked.

As Dora passed through the apple trees, they smelled different, sweeter somehow. Dora touched a red apple hanging from the nearest tree branch. It fell to the ground with a thud. She picked it up. It was bruised, and a worm crawled out of a hole it had made. Dora dropped the apple and continued out of the orchard. The swish of grass against her skirts was loud in the still air.

Dora snuck in behind Augusta's bower and waited, watching through a crack in the curtains. Inside, the lady sat on the edge of her bed. She hummed a song to herself and drummed an uneven rhythm on the bed frame. Her eyelids were heavy. Eventually, she lay down on the bed without undressing, then crawled in under a rose-colored duvet and closed her eyes. When her breaths had lengthened, Dora went around to the entrance and stepped inside.

Lady Augusta didn't look so scary in her sleep, tucked under her duvet. Her eyebrows were drawn together, as if she were considering something very hard. The bower was a mess of furniture, clothes, strange ornaments. In the center, a sloped table with some papers. Dora picked one up. It was a sketch of something with bristles and angles. There were more drawings under the first one: contraptions, buildings, something with wings, other things Dora couldn't name. A paper was covered in curlicued writing that must mean something. Perhaps it was important, but Dora couldn't read much except for her own name and Thistle's. None of them were there. She put the paper in her pinafore anyway and looked around. If it wasn't written down on paper, there must be something else here, somewhere the lady kept Thistle's name. Could it be engraved on a jewel in a box? Could it be as a breath in a jar? It must be kept very safe. But would she recognize it if she saw it? She had to try.

Augusta shifted in her sleep. Dora gingerly opened the drawers on the vanity, looked under chairs, in the folds of the wall hangings, and even lifted a corner of the mattress on the lady's bed. She found paint pots and little bird skulls and crystal ornaments, but nothing that looked like a name.

"Dora," a voice whispered.

It was Thistle. He stood in the doorway and looked at her with wide eyes. He made a come-here motion with his hand. Dora picked her way through the mess and joined him. Thistle tugged at her sleeve. Behind them, Augusta stirred and mumbled something Dora couldn't hear. Thistle broke into a run. Dora followed him.

When they entered the birch grove, out of sight from the bower, Thistle grabbed Dora's arms and stared up at her.

"What were you doing?" he hissed.

"I was looking for your name," Dora said. "I couldn't find it."

"I don't think it's a thing. If it was a thing, I would have stolen it while she was asleep," Thistle said. "I think I need her to speak it."

"Can we make her do that?" Dora asked.

"Don't you think I've tried?" Thistle replied. "I've tried to make her say it by accident. I've tried to bargain. I've tried everything."

"I could threaten her," Dora said. "I'm strong. I would do it for you."

"No, you can't," Thistle said. "She would use her voice. She would hurt you."

"She's not allowed to," Dora replied. "They don't hurt their own kind."

"She'd do something to you. Please don't give her the chance."

Thistle's eyes were tearing up. Dora could feel her own throat constrict.

"I don't want you to die. I would be all alone."

Thistle gave her a thin smile. "We'll think of something."

"What will you think of?" someone said.

Next to a birch tree stood a person who hadn't been there moments before: a very tall woman wrapped in robes and a flowing headscarf that seemed made of shifting shadows. Her long face was the purple shade of storm clouds, and her eyes shone yellow. She smiled, and the smile was sharp and toothy, but not unfriendly.

"Hello, Dora," she said, with a deep voice that crackled.

"Hello, Ghorbi," Dora replied.

Ghorbi walked over to where Dora and Thistle were standing. She raised one of her large hands and caressed Dora's cheek. When she spoke, her breath was hot and dry.

"I'm visiting the lady Mnemosyne on business, so I thought I'd have a look at you. You're almost a woman now. Nearly as tall as I. Big and strong, hair like white feathers, eyes dark as the earth. Truly a daughter of the mountain."

Her smile waned as she looked Dora over.

"You're filthy," she said. "Doesn't your father take care of you?"

"Thistle takes care of me," Dora said.

"Walpurgis doesn't want her," Thistle added.

Ghorbi looked down at Thistle. "Who are you, little page?"

"This is Thistle," Dora said. "I call him my brother."

"And why doesn't Walpurgis want you, Dora?" Ghorbi asked.

Dora looked down at her feet.

Ghorbi frowned. "Your father made a promise," she said. "If he didn't keep it, the deal is off. I fetched him his daughter, against payment and his promise to care for her. If he didn't, she would be free."

"Free?" Dora asked.

"I can show you the way out," Ghorbi said. "You can take care of yourself."

"I won't leave without Thistle," Dora said. "Augusta has his name."

Ghorbi tilted her head and frowned. "I can't do much about that," she said. "Thistle's case is none of my business. I'm sorry."

"Is there nothing you can do?" Thistle asked. "There must be something."

"I'm a trader, child," Ghorbi said. "I don't take sides. I can't interfere with an agreement that I'm not a part of, as much as it may sadden me. There are many terrible things in the multiverse, and it's not in my power to save everyone and everything."

"Have you seen what they do to us?" Thistle asked. "Have you really?"

"What do you mean?" Ghorbi said.

"They cut us," Thistle said. "Then they kill us and eat us. And Augusta is the worst of them. I will be next."

Ghorbi was quiet for a long moment, and the flame in her gaze intensified. Then she said, "I didn't know it was that bad."

"So do something," Thistle said. "Help us."

"I will listen and learn," Ghorbi said. "And see what I can see."

She patted Thistle's shoulder. "I must go. The lady Mnemosyne will be waking up soon."

The sharp note of a flute cut through the air: the first servant had woken up and signaled to the rest that it was time to prepare the next feast.

4

Lady Augusta straightened her coat and flipped her curled hair over her shoulders. She was standing with the others in the statuary grove where tonight's feast had been laid out. On the marble dais at the center, Mnemosyne sat on her throne. A high-backed chair stood next to the throne, on which sat that strange purple-faced woman, Ghorbi, wrapped in her shadowy robes. She and Mnemosyne were engaged in quiet conversation, heads leaning toward each other. Every so often, Ghorbi would look at the gathered nobles and flash them a jagged smile.

Everyone else was uncharacteristically quiet. They just didn't know what to say. Walpurgis fidgeted and drank from a bottle in his hand; Cymbeline and Virgilia were fiddling with each other's dresses; Euterpe was nervously clearing her throat. Mnemosyne acted as if Ghorbi was a regular guest, and she did seem familiar ... but at the same time profoundly alien.

Eventually, Mnemosyne drew away from Ghorbi and clapped her hands.

"My darlings!" she said. "It is time to dance. Let us show our guest how we celebrate youth and beauty."

As one, the crowd divided into two lines. A lively beat began to play, and the dancers joined hands across the divide. The party had begun.

All through the dance and the revels, Augusta kept an eye on Ghorbi. The traveler stayed in her seat next to the throne, watching the revelers with an expression that seemed amused and contemptuous at the same time. She knew things. Augusta was sure of it. Strange things. She must know about "time." As Mnemosyne left the dais to join the dance and the others gathered around her in a circle, Augusta walked away from the crowd and sidled up to the dais.

Ghorbi turned her face toward Augusta, and the pupils of her eyes reflected the lantern light.

"Who might you be, then?" she asked.

"I am the lady Augusta Prima," Augusta said, and inclined her head.

Ghorbi narrowed her eyes. "Augusta Prima. Your reputation precedes you."

Augusta smiled in satisfaction. "Of course."

"And what is on your mind, Augusta Prima?"

"I would like to have a conversation," Augusta said. "About things that you might know."

"Aha," Ghorbi replied.

Augusta looked at the dancers. "But not here. Would you come to my pavilion?"

Ghorbi nodded. "Yes."

"Follow the servant," Augusta said.

Some servant Augusta couldn't name stood at the edge of the dance floor with a tray in his hand. He twitched as Augusta came close.

"You will show the traveler to my bower," Augusta said. "Take a detour. I don't want the others to know where you're going. I will be waiting there for you."

"Yes, my lady," the servant said with his eyes fixed on the tray.

Augusta smoothed a stray lock of hair out of his face. "You look nice," she said. "Good."

"Thank you, my lady," the servant said.

Augusta flipped his tray over and left the dance floor.

It wasn't long before Ghorbi arrived. Standing up, she filled the doorway.

"What do you want to talk about?" she asked.

Augusta dug the locket out of her pocket and opened it. "This."

"Yes?" Ghorbi said.

"This is a watch."

"Yes."

"I have been trying to measure time here and there. Sometimes it passes, and sometimes it does not. Or perhaps it is the watch. I don't know."

Ghorbi was quiet for a second. Then she said, "Ah."

Augusta looked up at her. "I want you to tell me the truth about time and the world."

Ghorbi's mouth twisted into a smirk. "You might get in trouble."

"I need to know," Augusta said. "I cannot bear not knowing."

"Let me ask you for some information in return," Ghorbi said. "That is my price."

"Ask," Augusta replied.

"Thistle," Ghorbi said. "And the other children. Do you torture them?"

Augusta blinked. "Torture?"

"Torture," Ghorbi said. "Do you cut them?"

Augusta shrugged. "Of course. But it's not torture. It's art."

Ghorbi pursed her lips. "Does it not bother you that they are children?"

"They're *servants*," Augusta replied. "They belong to us."

"I see," Ghorbi said. "Very well. I have what I need."

"Your turn," Augusta said.

"Indeed," Ghorbi said, and beckoned Augusta closer. "Listen carefully."

When Ghorbi had left, Augusta felt faint. She sat down at her desk and grabbed a sheet of paper and a pen. She was in such a rush that she dribbled ink all over the paper. She filled sheet after sheet, everything she could find. When she had obliterated the pen nib, she grabbed a stick of charcoal and drew images of what Ghorbi had told her. It was all there. It all made sense.

"Augusta," someone said behind her. "My child."

Augusta twisted around in her chair. Mnemosyne stood in the middle of the room. Her ivy dress fluttered around her like branches in a breeze; the laurel wreath was tangled in her honey-colored hair. Never before had the lady visited Augusta's bower.

Augusta stood up. "My lady."

Mnemosyne regarded her in silence. Then she said, "This is a paradise, is it not?"

"It is, my lady," Augusta replied.

"It is," Mnemosyne echoed. She tilted her head. "Then why are the apples going bad, Augusta?"

Augusta faltered. "I haven't noticed, my lady."

"I have. My mind . . . is not quite always there. But I see it."

"I don't understand, my lady."

"Ghorbi told me, you see," Mnemosyne said. "She came to me and told me. What you have been doing. She said you wanted to know about the world outside. And time. Why do you want to know about those things, Augusta?"

"I . . ." Augusta gestured at the pile of paper behind her. "I was curious."

Mnemosyne took a step forward. Augusta saw now that her round face was streaked with tears.

"You helped me build this place. That fact will never leave my mind. So it is like tearing my own heart out, Augusta," she said. "But you must go."

She laid a hand on Augusta's forehead.

"I will not let anything threaten this realm. Farewell."

5

Dora walked back through the orchard. The trees closest to the conservatory sagged with rotting fruit. Maggots fed on the fallen apples around their trunks. This had never happened before, not that Dora had ever seen.

The conservatory's thick glass had cracked in places; branches and vines had burst out to climb the broken surface. For the first time, the dome's little door was ajar. The rich smell of cooking wafted out. Dora crouched down and crawled inside.

The Aunts looked strange where they lay on their couches. They looked lumpy, sunken in on themselves. As Dora crept closer, it became clear that these were not the Aunts. It was just their skin, neatly peeled off their bodies and laid out. Swaddled in the skins lay the three Nieces, fast asleep. On the floor next to each couch sat a human-shaped cake on a small porcelain plate. They looked like the little figures the Nieces otherwise would scoop out from the Aunts' chests, but they weren't moving.

Dora picked up a cake. It smelled of meat pie, and she was reminded that she hadn't eaten in a long time. Dora bent over the nearest Niece to listen for her breath and heard none. She would not need this cake. Dora ate it. It tasted of lard and salt. She ate the second one, too, and the third, then sat down. The cakes made her sleepy. The conservatory was very quiet, so quiet that her ears buzzed. Dora made her mind empty.

Someone knocked on the glass. It was Thistle. Dora opened the door, and Thistle wrinkled his nose and waved a hand in front of his face as she stepped outside.

"What are you doing in here?" he asked.

"The Aunts aren't growing back," Dora said.

Thistle frowned. "They always grow back."

"Augusta was here when you were sleeping," Dora said. "She had that locket. I think she did something to them."

"She did indeed." Ghorbi stood a few steps away, gazing past Dora into the conservatory.

"What's going on?" Thistle asked.

Ghorbi looked amused more than anything.

"Change," Ghorbi said. She walked up to the dome and ran a hand down the glass. "Augusta called on me while I was meeting with Lady Mnemosyne. It seems she has been experimenting, with interesting results. Time has begun to pass again."

"What happens now?" Thistle asked.

"Augusta damaged this world," Ghorbi said. "She and her little contraption have been cast out so that the place can heal."

Thistle looked stricken. "She's gone?"

Ghorbi nodded.

"She can't be," Thistle said.

"I thought you'd be pleased," Ghorbi said. "She can't hurt you now. She is not here, so you are no longer under her sway. You can go anywhere you wish."

"But she still has my name," Thistle said. "I can't find my way back home until I have my name. I have to go after her."

Ghorbi frowned. "And get it from her . . . how exactly? She's a dangerous woman and even out of here has powerful magic."

"I don't know!" Thistle shouted. "There has to be a way."

Ghorbi looked over Dora's shoulder and raised her eyebrows at what she saw.

"Ah," she said.

They came walking through the apple trees: Cymbeline, Virgilia, Walpurgis, Tempestis, and Euterpe. Their powdered faces were almost luminescent in the gloom, their rich silks and satins rustling like the wind in the trees.

"Thistle," Walpurgis said, and his voice was oily. "Your mistress is gone, and we are hungry."

Next to him, Cymbeline raised a curved knife. "We can't have stray servants running about."

Dora stepped in front of Thistle. "You can't have him."

Walpurgis laughed. "Oh, but we can. Get out of the way, monster."

Dora felt herself moving aside against her will.

"Enough," Ghorbi said.

Virgilia fixed her eyes on Ghorbi. "Don't meddle in our affairs, outsider. You don't belong here."

Ghorbi grabbed Dora and Thistle by the hand. "With me."

Behind them, a shrill cry went up, followed by a chorus of baying voices. Ghorbi ran with impossibly long steps, so fast that Dora had to push herself to keep up. As they ran, Ghorbi opened her mouth. A long, low note grew in her chest and emerged from her lips. It reverberated in the air and somehow harmonized with itself, then became a word, two syllables repeated over and over again. The note climbed higher, and the air trembled. A breeze stirred.

As they reached the pine trees that guarded the edge of the orchard, the wind intensified, nearly drowning out the sound of Ghorbi's voice. The cold air raked at Dora's face like needles. It occurred to her that it wasn't just wind but sand, and it obscured the trees from view. A whirling inferno of sand enveloped them. Then the wind died down, and Ghorbi's song faded, and with a thud, they landed on something solid.

They were elsewhere.

PART II

OUTSIDE

6

Augusta woke up with a stiff neck. She had fallen asleep sitting down, her head resting on a pile of scribbled notes. When she straightened, she found herself at her old drafting table, but it stood beneath a window in a small room with wooden walls. A narrow bed with tattered sheets filled the rest of the space. On the other side of the window stood a forest, bathed in light.

A golden chain hung from her waistcoat pocket. She swung the locket into her hand. It was ticking in a steady rhythm, not haltingly like in the Gardens. Forward, ever forward.

The sheets of paper that littered the desk were filled with inky blotches and random words in indigo and sepia. Augusta could not make sense of them. What was it Ghorbi had told her? It was difficult to think.

Next to the desk was a door with a curled handle. Augusta got up from the chair and opened it. Unbearable light rushed over her. She backed inside and slammed the door. The sun. She was not in the Gardens anymore.

Augusta crawled in under the covers on the bed. The blanket couldn't quite block out the light, but at least Augusta's eyes didn't hurt. She lay there, listening to the ticking of the watch, until she lost count.

Eventually, the light faded and that awful orb sank behind the treetops. Augusta waited until the darkness was almost complete. She stepped outside again and looked at the tiny cottage behind her. Where was she? The air was different here, cold and crisp. The warble of blackbirds had died down, and bright pinpricks filled the sky. Stars, where the sky ought to have been smooth and empty. And there, floating above the trees, a swollen moon. Bile rose in Augusta's throat. Just like the sun, that thing was an aberration.

A little track led into the depths of the forest. This was not so different from the forest that surrounded the Gardens. Perhaps she was close after all.

She lost the trail almost immediately, stumbling over rocks and tree roots. The smell of the night forest filled her nose: pine needles, decomposing leaves, damp earth. Somewhere, an animal let out a barking noise. Nearby, something else hooted.

"Euterpe!" she called. "Mnemosyne! Walpurgis!"

At first it seemed that the light was just right, a familiar blue that erased all shadows, soft on the eye. Augusta thought that she could see the conservatory's great dome just beyond the trees, and her heart lifted.

"Euterpe!" she shouted. "I'm here!"

She ran through the forest, her chest burning with every breath. Twigs whipped at her sides, and once she stumbled and scraped her knee. She got back up and forced herself to run faster, away from the world, toward safety.

But then birds began to sing, and as the light grew, the tree trunks all around took on a hard silhouette. Then the trees abruptly ended. Before her, a great plain spread out, rolling fields that smelled of manure and dewy growth. Ahead, what she thought had been the conservatory's dome. It was the top of a tower. On a hill in the middle of the plain sat a great castle, peachy pink in the morning light. Beyond the castle, the two tall spires of a cathedral soared into the sky. A city sprawled beneath them. It all tugged at something in Augusta's mind. She had seen a city like this before, and she had loathed it.

Augusta looked over her shoulder at the forest, backlit now by the rising sun. Mnemosyne had truly cast her out. How dare she?

There must be a way back into the Gardens. Perhaps this place would have some answers. At least there would be food and drink. Augusta would return to the Gardens, and return in triumph. Nil desperandum. She began to walk.

Augusta walked past fields and farms along a gravel road that eventually became a cobbled street. She continued in among one- and two-story stone houses that were occasionally interrupted by wooden cottages. Save for an odd roar in the distance, the street was quiet. A woman emerged from one of the houses and crossed the road in front of Augusta; she was wearing a knee-length coat of an odd, formless cut and a drab little hat. Her calves were scandalously bare. Even so, her posture and colors made Augusta think of wood lice. The woman glanced over her shoulder at Augusta and stumbled over her own feet. Augusta chuckled but was interrupted when she saw a man rolling down the street astride a wheeled contraption. A woman followed him on another thing just like it. Augusta stared at them in fascination. Then the aroma of baking bread hit her like a wave.

The shop sat on a corner. On the other side of the window, a man kneaded an enormous lump of dough while a girl took out tray after tray of cakes from a large oven. Augusta tried the door. It was locked. She banged on the glass pane. The girl took off her oven mittens and came to open it. She looked up at Augusta with large, mottled eyes in a slim face.

"We're closed," she said.

"You will open for me," Augusta told her in her lady voice, as when addressing a servant, and watched with satisfaction as the girl's mouth slackened and her eyes became glassy.

"Of course," the girl said after a moment. "Come inside."

In the little space, there was a counter and a glass cabinet filled to the brim with cakes. The smells in here made Augusta's mouth water: bread, baking fruits, spices.

"I want one of everything, and water," she told the girl.

The girl obediently took out a small box and filled it, then filled a glass bottle with water and set them both on the counter.

"Good girl," Augusta said.

Augusta left with the box and the bottle in her arms. The houses rose higher, stately with elaborate facades. Twice, foul-smelling carriages roared past her, seemingly without anything to pull them. More and more people emerged into the street. They were doughy and mundane little things, most of them with skin like sand, fair or auburn hair sticking out from under the brim of lumpy hats or headscarves. The women walked around in more of those scandalously short dresses that displayed their legs, which would have been interesting if said dresses were not in such excruciatingly dull shades; the men wore ill-fitting short jackets and long trousers. They stared at Augusta. Augusta stared back. She sat down on a bench under a tree to drink the water and eat the pastries. They were delicate and crumbly, some of them filled with berries, others twisted into elaborate shapes. The sun blazed overhead, but Augusta was slowly getting used to it. She let it warm her shoulders as she watched the people passing by. When she was finished, she left the bottle and box on the bench.

This place was familiar, and yet not. She had hated a place like this and could not say exactly why, but she had her suspicions. It was noisy and smelly and crowded. There were parks, but the trees were stunted and manicured. The paved streets were disturbed by horses and carts, rattling vehicles, and above all, people. The river that flowed through the city looked muddy and cold. And yet, Augusta found herself intrigued. All around her, people scurried like mice, like insects, giving her a wide berth. She wandered the streets until the light softened and her feet hurt.

There was a side street of rose-trellised wooden houses, away from the hustle and bustle. One of the houses had a door embossed with flowers, and two little porcelain dogs sat in the window. Augusta climbed the steps to the door and pushed down the handle. It was unlocked.

She stepped into a room. An old woman in a dress and an apron was stirring a pot on a stove. A younger woman sat at a table by the window, darning socks. They both looked up as Augusta entered.

"Who are you?" said the older woman. "What are you doing here?"

"I'm going to live here now," Augusta said. "What are your names?"

The younger woman was meek. "My name is Elsa," she said.

The crone frowned and walked over to where Augusta was standing.

"You won't have my name," she said. "Get out. You're not welcome here."

Augusta drew herself up and stared at the woman. "Do as I say."

"I . . ." the crone said, and faltered.

"You're going to be trouble," Augusta said.

She put her hands around the old woman's throat and squeezed. When her victim had stopped struggling, she turned to the girl.

"Elsa. You are my maid now."

Elsa dragged her mother's corpse into a chamber next to the kitchen. She sobbed all the while, but she did not resist Augusta. She showed Augusta to a small room with a bathtub, which she filled with warm water that miraculously came out of the wall.

"How marvelous," Augusta said. "How does that work?"

"It's just water," Elsa mumbled. "I don't know."

While Augusta washed herself, she made Elsa answer questions. The city was called Uppsala, and someone named Gustaf the Fifth was king. A country called Germany was making war, invading its neighbors. The Germans might come here or they might not. Times were hard.

When Augusta had dried off, Elsa showed her into a larger bedchamber and opened an armoire. Augusta waved away the flimsy dresses Elsa presented her with. Finally, Elsa opened another door and took out a black suit of the same strange cut Augusta had seen the men wear in the street.

"This was Father's Sunday best," Elsa said, and her eyes watered a little.

"It will do," Augusta said, and put it on.

She looked at herself in the mirror on the armoire's door. It showed a woman completely devoid of interesting details and scents. Her hair was still wet and hung almost straight down. And her face, her face. Pages had always adorned it with artful designs, to suit a noble of good taste. Without them, her face seemed empty: the round eyes had no edges, the broad cheekbones that invited swirls lay bare; her mouth was like a half-healed wound. No lord or lady even in their most extravagant stupors had ever gone with a naked face.

"Where are your paints?" Augusta demanded.

"I have this," Elsa said, and held up a stick of fuchsia-colored wax.

"It will do," Augusta said, and rubbed some onto strategic spots. Much better.

"Now feed me," she told Elsa. "Then tell me where to find learned men and women."

7

They found themselves on a cracked plain that stretched out in all directions. The sand had disappeared, and Dora was standing on mud that had dried and split. The sky above them was wide like a fishpond. Something like an inverted sun hung up there, an empty disc surrounded by a blinding corona. Thistle had sat down on the ground, panting heavily, elbows resting on his knees. He gave Dora a strained smile as she crouched next to him.

"What happens now?" Thistle said from the ground.

"I couldn't let them have you," Ghorbi said. "And I can't just leave you here. This is a crossroads between worlds."

Thistle stood up. He was almost breathing normally now. "You can take us to where Augusta is."

"I suppose I could, theoretically," Ghorbi said. "Except I don't know where she went. Possibly to Earth, from whence you all came. Possibly to one of the other realms. But there are many, so many. She may have ended up anywhere." She tapped her chin with a long fingernail. "I could direct you to someone who might help you."

"Do it," Dora said. "Please."

Ghorbi was quiet for a moment. "I don't hand out favors left and right. I have already helped Thistle twice, out of the goodness of my heart. But everything comes with a price."

"We have nothing," Thistle said.

Ghorbi looked down at him, and her eyes flickered. "Will you repay me later?"

Thistle nodded. "Yes. Anything."

"Anything," Ghorbi said. "I will keep this in mind."

Ghorbi strode off toward a structure in the distance. Dora and Thistle followed. She could see the silhouettes of people.

"Is that where Augusta is?" Thistle asked.

"No. This is where you come to go somewhere else."

Inside a chest-high stone enclosure, wooden stalls were lined up in two neat rows. At each table, a strange-looking person was busy pressing buttons on a box or writing on paper and tablets. The people were bald, with skin that reminded Dora of ashes; their eyes were huge and their limbs long. They were swaddled in lengths of gauzy, colorless fabric. Very long toes peeked out from under the hem of their robes.

When Dora and Thistle caught up with Ghorbi, she was waiting in front of one of the tables. On it sat a sphere as big as Dora's head, out of which keys stuck out at odd angles. The person behind the desk was busy with the sphere, muttering to itself.

"Who are they?" Dora asked.

"Traffic controllers," Ghorbi said. "They direct whoever comes here to where they need to go." She smiled. "They have always been here. Perhaps they are little gods. Benign ones, mind you."

The traffic controller finished whatever it was doing, then looked up at Ghorbi and nodded. It spoke a long stream of crisp syllables in a hoarse voice. Ghorbi replied in the same language. The other pointed at Dora and Thistle. Ghorbi said something else, the tone of her voice rising at the end of the sentence. She got a single vowel in reply.

Thistle sat down on the ground again.

Dora sank down next to him and put her arm around his shoulders. "Are you tired?"

"I feel like I haven't slept for days. And I'm hungry and thirsty."

Thistle rested his head against her shoulder. Dora closed her eyes and let the sounds wash over her: talk, clicks, quills rasping on paper.

She came to with a start when Ghorbi touched her shoulder.

"It's time to go," Ghorbi said.

Thistle rubbed his eyes. "Where are we going?"

"I asked them if they've seen Augusta, but she hasn't been through here. I couldn't find out where she is now, but I know of some people who might be able to locate her. I'll show you to the realm where you might find them."

Ghorbi helped Dora and Thistle to their feet.

"We're hungry," Dora said.

Ghorbi paused. "Ah." She went over to one of the stalls and conferred with one of the traffic controllers, then came back.

"They are willing to sell you food," she said. "For a price. It's steep. Direction is free, but food isn't."

"We don't have anything to pay them with," Thistle said.

Ghorbi nodded at Dora. "They want your hair."

"Oh," Dora said.

"Are you very attached to it?"

Dora shrugged.

"Dora, no," Thistle said.

"I'm hungry," Dora replied. "So are you."

"Come," Ghorbi said.

Dora followed her. At the stall, the traffic controller babbled excitedly and took out a very sharp-looking knife. Up close, the creature smelled like smoke. It grabbed hold of Dora's hair and deftly cut it off, strand after white strand, close to her scalp. When it was done, a neatly ordered heap of hair lay on the table. Dora touched her head. It felt light, free. Next to her, Thistle looked devastated.

"You're bald," he said.

Dora laughed. "I like this," she said. "It feels good."

The traffic controller nodded and gathered Dora's hair into a small box, then bent down and rummaged under the table. It placed an opaque bottle and an object wrapped in waxy paper in front of Dora. It bowed and said something.

"This is from its private stores," Ghorbi said. "It offers the food to you with many thanks."

Dora opened the package. It contained what looked like a cake. She broke off a piece and put it in her mouth. It was chewy and tasted vaguely like dried fruit. She handed another piece to Thistle.

"It's all right," she said.

Thistle hesitated, then crammed the cake into his mouth.

The liquid in the bottle was water with a metallic taste. Dora drank half of it and gave the rest to Thistle. She felt better. Thistle looked better, too.

"Now, then," Ghorbi said. "Let's go."

They walked to another opening in the wall, and through it onto the baked-mud plain.

"It looks just the same," Dora said.

"Does it?"

Ghorbi pointed at the ground. A single blade of yellow grass stuck up, waving in a faint breeze.

"This is as far as I go. Just keep walking in that direction, straight ahead, until you see tall trees and statues guarding a city made of stone. You are looking for a theater troupe. They come there often."

Thistle frowned. "But why aren't you coming with us?"

Ghorbi shook her head. "The people you are about to see won't welcome me."

"Why?" Thistle asked.

"It's a long story." Ghorbi smiled wistfully. "Once upon a time, I saved one of them. He fell in love with me and wanted me to stay. But I am a traveler, and so I left, and it broke his heart. He has been angry ever since."

"I'm sorry," Thistle said.

Ghorbi chuckled. "Don't be sorry for me. He's the one who couldn't let go. That's why I don't hand out favors anymore. It creates bonds that are hard to break."

She kissed each of them on the forehead. "You'll do just fine. If ever there is an emergency, sing the song I sang, and it will bring you here. Do you remember it?"

Thistle nodded.

"Good," Ghorbi said. "Now go."

8

Augusta found her way to the university, which Elsa had said was populated by scholars. She wandered the grounds, cornering students and professors, until three officious-looking men told her to leave. Too much attention might not be good. These people were no use anyway; no one knew of the Gardens, and no one was an adept of the mystical arts.

Instead, she took to the streets at night, when the air smelled of damp stone and dewy flowers. She walked through the cemetery, where mausoleums and proud obelisks spoke of poets and philosophers. She climbed the stairs to the castle and waited for the rising sun to tint its towers rose. Then she went back to her house with the flowery door and slept.

It went on like this for a few days and nights: days spent sleeping, nights spent walking. Until, as she sat for the sunrise by the castle, the bench shifted under the weight of another person.

"You look lost, madam."

The voice was a mellow tenor or an alto, neither particularly male nor female. It belonged to a slender figure impeccably dressed in a three-piece tweed suit and a hat with a rounded crown. The stranger's skin was smooth and lustrous in the morning light, like a well-thumbed leather book cover, and lay in deep folds between nose and mouth. Despite the fact that they had addressed her formally, there was something eerily frank about how they looked at her.

"Perhaps," Augusta replied.

The stranger nodded. "For how long?"

Augusta shrugged.

"Not sure?" the stranger said. "I have seen you walking around town," they continued. "Wandering, always wandering. I followed you here. You look out of place. Where are you from?"

Augusta scoffed. "What would you know? Go away."

She had used her lady voice, and yet the stranger didn't move.

"That kind of magic will not work on me," they said calmly. "Now, where are you from?"

The stranger's gaze was much too direct. Augusta had an impulse to poke their eyes out. The stranger's hand on her own made her aware that she had actually almost done so.

"I am a lady of the Gardens," Augusta said. "Unhand me."

The stranger's hand squeezed hers a little, enough that she could feel that it was much stronger than her own, then let go. "You are not the first to pass through," they said.

Augusta shrunk back, cradling her hand. "That's not nice," she muttered.

The stranger merely smiled. "You will have to control yourself better. One can't assault people if one doesn't like what they're doing here. Not me, nor anyone else."

Augusta blinked. "Why?"

"It can get you in trouble. Now, for introductions." The stranger tipped their hat. "You may call me Pinax."

"I see," Augusta said.

Pinax looked at her expectantly.

"You may call me the Most Honorable Augusta Prima," Augusta said. "And you may address me as 'your ladyship.'"

"I would prefer not to, but fair enough."

Augusta snorted. Pinax seemed to be waiting for her to speak. She forced herself to sit still on the bench, that thing which was called waiting. Stay and do nothing while time passed. All this time that ran off and disappeared. She could feel her body rotting from the inside out.

"You say I am not the first," she said eventually, mostly because she couldn't bear the silence anymore.

Pinax nodded. "That's right, your ladyship."

"I know nothing of anyone leaving."

"That's the nature of your people, though, isn't it? To not remember. To live the same evening over and over again."

Augusta drew herself up. "I remember."

"How much?"

"I found a thing under the dog-rose bush . . ." She hesitated.

Pinax waited, quietly.

"A thing under the dog-rose bush," Augusta repeated, lamely. "I found a corpse. It had a watch."

"And then?"

"I showed the watch to my page, and he told me about time. And I wanted to see if time really passed in the Gardens."

"And did it?"

"The watch moved," Augusta said. "Here and there. And then the lady Mnemosyne found me in my bower. And then I was here. *She banished me.*" The enormity of it.

"I see. And do you remember the beginning of the Gardens?" said Pinax.

A jumble of parties. Drinking, dancing. Beyond that, a void. The *before.* Augusta crossed her arms and stared up at the castle.

"This is familiar," she said. "A city, much like this. But also very different."

They sat in silence.

"He called himself Phantasos," Pinax said eventually. "I found him right here, under the lilac. He said he was the lord of the Gardens."

Augusta scoffed. "There is no lord of the Gardens. Mnemosyne is our lady."

"Ah. Mnemosyne. Yes. He was her consort."

"Where is this Phantasos?"

"He left."

"Where is he? I need to find him. If he left of his own free will, he could take me back."

"He has another life now," Pinax said.

The moment was still. Augusta tried to move, but it was still the same. It sat on her like a stone, making it hard to breathe.

"It's difficult, isn't it," Pinax said. "Being outside."

"Yes," she managed.

Pinax took her hand. "Come."

Augusta didn't have the energy to pull away.

Pinax led her down the hill from the castle. The city was waking up again. Eventually they turned onto a street where linden trees rose up beside granite buildings, and the noise of traffic died down. Pinax stopped outside a two-story stone house nestled between two taller buildings.

"This is where I live," Pinax said, and unlocked the heavy door.

Augusta stepped into darkness. Her feet echoed on marble. Pinax flicked a switch on the wall, and the space flooded with yellow light. They stood in a long, narrow corridor lined with doors on either side. Pinax walked ahead to the end of the hallway and opened a door.

"Here," they said, and motioned Augusta inside.

The room was entirely lined with books. Augusta had never seen so many: fat volumes, slender notebooks, tiny books, and huge folios, all ordered in neat rows. On an ornate carpet stood two leather armchairs and a small table. The plush chaise longue under the room's single window was covered in rolled-up manuscripts.

"Please, have a seat," Pinax said. "I'll make us some tea."

Augusta sank down in a chair as Pinax left. She could hear them walk back down the hallway and then into another room, where they made tea-making noises: a whistling kettle, the pouring of hot water into a pot, cups and saucers bumping together. After not too long, they returned with a tray with a teapot and two cups, and a plate of plain bread and cheese. Augusta picked up a slice of bread and bit into it. It was bland and slid down her gullet only reluctantly. She dropped the rest on the floor.

Pinax frowned. "That's not acceptable in my house. Please don't do that again."

"Bring me something else," Augusta said.

"I am not your servant," Pinax said. "Please pick up the bread."

"You do it," Augusta said.

"You are a guest," Pinax said. "You have stepped over my threshold and eaten my food. You'll have to abide by my rules."

Augusta felt the blood drain from her face. She had eaten the bread without thinking.

Pinax leaned back in their chair. "This is my domain."

Augusta found herself bending down and picking up the piece of bread. "Who are you?"

Pinax gave her a level look. "Perhaps when I feel so inclined, I might tell you a story. For now, my patience has run out. You may leave."

Augusta got out of the chair. Pinax nodded at her. She left the house without daring to look back.

9

The sky clouded over until it lay over the plain like a flat lid. Thick yellow grass reached to Dora's knees. The terrain wasn't quite level anymore but had bumps and hollows in which water gathered.

Thistle kneeled by the closest hollow and scooped some water into his cupped hands. Dora crouched down next to him. The water was tasteless and clear. It was as if someone had poured it there just now.

Thistle washed his face, smoothed back his locks, and buttoned his coat with shivering hands. His makeup had smeared everywhere. He produced a handkerchief from his breast pocket and dipped it in the water, then rubbed it over Dora's face.

"You've got crumbs and sand all over."

Dora took the handkerchief from him. "You've got paint all over," she said.

She scrubbed his face until it was pink and raw but clean. He looked like a new person.

"You have freckles," Dora observed. "And stubble."

Thistle felt his jaw. "I do."

He caught her hand and held it against his face for a moment. His skin felt like rough velvet.

Thistle sighed into her hand and turned his eyes to the plain. "How far do we have to walk?"

"Straight ahead, like she said."

"But what if we get turned around? What then?"

"We ask someone."

"How do we even know there are people out there we can ask, Dora?"

"I don't know."

"But what if we . . ."

"Stop." Dora let her hand fall. "We don't know. It's all right."

"You don't seem worried at all," Thistle said.

"I'm good at not knowing," Dora replied.

There was a line on the horizon. They walked toward it.

Eventually, they came to a lake with a stone beach. It was so big that Dora couldn't see the other side. In the distance on their left, a tower stuck out of the waterline. As they came closer, it became clear that it was a ruin, built out of something that looked like crumbly stone. There was a ground floor and a second floor, but the roof was gone. Rods stuck out of the top at crooked angles. A half-submerged opening faced the lake. Dora picked up her skirts and waded into the water. It was cool against her legs, the shingle under her feet smooth and slippery.

"It's too cold," Thistle said from the waterline.

Dora looked over her shoulder. "Not for me."

"Be careful!" he called after her.

The room inside was empty. Snatches of pictures were stuck to the walls here and there: a sun, the profile of a woman cradling a child, a row of clenched fists. At the back of the room was a doorway, corked with debris from where the ceiling had collapsed. Next to it, a set of stairs led up.

On the next floor, two corridor stumps stretched out like a V under the bare sky. The left one had fallen in on itself to cover the door below. Dora turned right. The floor ended after just a few steps. In the room below, heaps of debris stuck out of the clear water. There was no sign of life: no moss, no lichen, no fish swimming in the ruin. Dora picked up a lump of rock and dropped it into the water. It made a loud splash that echoed against the walls.

"Anything?" Thistle called as she waded back outside.

Dora shook her head and made her way back to the shore. Thistle knelt and wrung out her skirts. She had forgotten to hike them up on the way back.

"I don't understand how you're not freezing." He shook the water off his hands and stuck them in his armpits.

"Are you cold?"

Thistle nodded.

Dora wiggled one of his hands free, then turned her back to him and put his hand on her shoulder.

"Come on," she said, and squatted. "Get up."

"I'm not that little anymore."

"Get up," Dora repeated.

Thistle sighed and climbed onto her back. She hooked her arms under his knees and walked up into the grass, then set off along the shore, the lake on her right-hand side.

÷

In the distance, a black thread lay stretched across the plain. One end disappeared into the water, the other continued as far as Dora could see. When they came closer, it became clear that it was some sort of pipe, big enough that Dora could have crawled inside. Inland, on the horizon, stood what looked like domes lit from within. Thistle hopped down from Dora's back and walked beside her toward the buildings.

Closer up, the domes looked like puffy beetles; beyond them stood squat buildings with tiny windows. In the center rose a tall tower, like the one by the lake but bigger and whole. People moved between the structures. They were dressed for work, in flat earthy shades, walking with their faces turned downward. One of them glanced up as Dora and Thistle approached, and let out a thin scream. Others looked up, too, and stared at them with wide eyes. They all retreated.

Thistle halted. "They don't want us here," he said.

"Could this be the help Ghorbi talked about?" Dora took a few more steps.

"I don't know if . . ." Thistle said, and then grabbed Dora's arm. "Look."

A small group came walking out between the domes: four men and women, armed with poles and shovels. They stopped a little distance away, close enough that Dora could see their angry faces.

"Who are you?" a short woman shouted.

"I'm Dora," said Dora loudly.

Thistle poked at her arm. "Dora, don't."

One of the men leaned over and mumbled something in the

short woman's ear. She shook her head and stepped closer. Her face was furrowed; her eyes were sharp.

"You don't belong here," she said, "do you." Her accent was nasal and choppy.

"We mean no harm," Thistle said. "We're just looking for someone."

The woman looked over her shoulder at the others, who shook their heads and made waving motions with their hands.

"You won't find anything here," the woman said.

"We're looking for some people," Dora said. "A theater troupe. They're supposed to help us."

"No one here but us," the woman replied. "You're not here either. You don't belong. You're not real."

"Please," Thistle said, and took a step toward the woman.

The woman raised her pole as if to hit him. Dora stepped between them. She tore the pole from the woman's hands and snapped it in two. The woman gasped and retreated.

Dora looked down at her. "You won't touch him."

The woman broke into a run. Dora and Thistle watched as the three others raced after her.

"How did you do that?" Thistle asked. "You're so strong."

"I am," Dora agreed. "I couldn't protect you properly against the lords and ladies. I will protect you here."

"We won't find out if Augusta is there," Thistle said.

"They said she wasn't."

"They could be lying."

The short woman was coming back. She had more people with her this time. Dora planted her feet on the ground, ready to defend herself and Thistle.

"They're too many," Thistle said. "Let's go."

÷

The crowd didn't follow. Dora and Thistle continued walking along the waterline until they reached a tongue of land. The stones were bigger there, and a pile of them formed a sort of wind shelter. Dora sat down to inspect her feet. They seemed all right, if a little sore. Thistle leaned back against the rock and hugged his knees. They sat in silence for a while, until the water changed.

It happened in time with the approaching twilight. With a crackling noise, tendrils spread across the water like a web, until they became so many that they covered the surface completely. Then the surface suddenly cleared. In the ebbing light, it looked absolutely black.

Dora tried the ice with her foot. It made a dull noise as she banged her heel against it. It was cold, but not terribly so. She thought she could see a shimmer in the distance. It looked almost like a string of starry sky.

"We could walk on this," Dora said.

So they did.

They came to the end of the cloud cover, and a sudden spray of stars glimmered in the heavens. A huge striped sphere hung up there, bigger than Dora's fist.

"I have a memory," Thistle suddenly said. "It was cold, and I was on a frozen lake. There was a little round hole in the ice. I think we were fishing."

"Who are 'we'?" Dora asked.

"I don't know," Thistle replied. "My parents, maybe."

He sniffled abruptly. "I want to go home."

"That's where we're going," Dora said. "We'll get you home."
She took his hand. It was cold.

"I'm going to pick you up again," she said. "You're freezing."
Thistle didn't protest.

As they walked across the ice, the sky changed color and a light rose up around the horizon, as if someone had lit an enormous lamp under the earth. Ahead of them lay a shore where the yellow grass grew all the way down to the water. As the light flowed into the sky and the striped giant faded to a shadow, thunder split the air. A long crack ran through the ice in front of them.

"Put me down," Thistle said, and struggled out of Dora's grasp. As he landed, a network of cracks spread around his feet.

"Oh no," he said.

The ice shivered, and Dora lost her balance. She landed on her back so hard that the air whooshed out of her lungs. Thistle yanked at her arm.

"We have to go!" he shouted. "Now!"

Dora fought for breath and managed to get up. Ahead of her, Thistle slid like a dancer across ice that cracked and groaned. She followed him at a slower pace; what had been rough and easy to walk on had now become wet and slick.

They had made it almost all the way to dry land when Dora's foot broke through. She slipped and fell forward, catching herself with her hands, but her legs slid down into the cold water until she was up to her chest. She could feel the stony bottom with her feet. Dora hammered on the ice in front of her, breaking it into pieces so she could wade forward. Thistle managed to skip across the last ice sheets and landed on the shore, where he collapsed. Dora hauled herself out of the water. Thistle touched her leg apologetically. Dora shrugged and blew at her palms. They sat on the grass, panting, watching the ice melt.

Thistle stood up and peered out across the plain that stretched out ahead of them, then up at the sky.

"Day and night," he said. "I remember day and night from when I was little. There should be a sun. Or a moon. I don't know what that is." He pointed at the sphere that loomed above them.

"I know," Dora said. "When Ghorbi came to get me. It was morning, and we walked until night fell. I saw the sun and the moon."

"We need to move on," Thistle said. "We need something to eat."

He was shivering.

"You're not all right," Dora observed.

Thistle let out a small laugh. "I'm really not," he agreed. "I'm hungry and I think I'm freezing to death."

"But it's warmer here," Dora said.

"Is it? I can't tell."

Dora hauled him onto her back. "Up you come."

She felt the hunger, too, but it was just one of those physical things, like her cold feet and Thistle's weight. She could keep going for a long time yet.

10

Elsa was asleep when Augusta came back. Augusta kicked her awake so she could have some tea. The girl was slow, too slow. Insolent. Augusta strangled her, just like she had her mother, and dragged her into the small chamber. She realized belatedly that finding another servant might be a trial. But her encounter with Pinax had left her in a foul temper.

She slept for a while, tossing and turning in the daylight that filtered through the curtains. When night fell, she did not go outside. She sat by the window, watching the quiet street and toying with one of the porcelain dogs. Pinax knew things. And they spoke to her like an equal, which was eerie and infuriating but an interesting change. Perhaps she should go back and play by their rules and see where that took her. They might tell her where Phantasos had gone. And if she could find Phantasos, she might find a way home. But everything had a price. An exchange would have to be made. A gift might put Pinax in better spirits.

When dawn broke, Augusta went to the bakery and ordered the shopgirl to fill a box with the cakes that had the most beautiful names. Then she found her way back to Pinax's house. They opened the door after a long moment. They were dressed in a paisley dressing gown.

"It's very early," they said.

Augusta held the box out. "I brought you a gift."

Pinax tilted their head. "So you did."

"May I come in?"

They looked Augusta up and down, then nodded. "You may."

Pinax showed her to the same room they had been in previously. "Wait here," they said.

Augusta walked along the bookshelves, peering at the volumes, while Pinax once again clinked porcelain in the distance. The books had titles that spoke of poetry, philosophy, and mythology. Some of them looked ancient, the leather covers cracked and the titles unreadable.

"It is a nice gesture," Pinax said behind her. "I take it manners do not come easily to you."

They stood behind her with a tray. They had dressed themself in the same suit as yesterday.

"You like books," Augusta said.

Pinax smiled. "I am a librarian, after all." They set the tray down on the table between the armchairs. "You wanted to know who I am. Since you came with a gift, I will tell you a story. Please sit."

Once upon a time there was a library. This wasn't just any library, but the library of a capital, older than the current royal dynasty, older than memory. It was built out of burnt brick, ancient but unmarked by the passage of time. Inside was a warren of rooms full of bookcases and shelves stacked with clay tablets, scrolls, codices, planks of wood, sticks, pieces of bone, and turtle shell. There were wax rolls on which were recorded oral histories and chants that could not be written down, because the notes and overtones also affected the language and changed its meaning in a way that couldn't be described in writing. There were librarians who served as living books, reciting stories that could be told only in gestures or dance. New material arrived with couriers each day. It was the greatest repository of literature in the known world.

The queen of this country was the last of a great dynasty. She came from a tradition of taking good care of literature. Her father had revered the library, and so had his mother before him. The queen sent out messengers and merchants to find new books; to collect all the literature mankind had produced. And she succeeded.

The library was an ecosystem of sorts; the sheer mass of the place couldn't help but produce life. Out of the collected knowledge, of the love with which the librarians and visitors treated the books, of the fossilized voices of a hundred thousand scribes and storytellers, little guardian spirits took form.

These keepers were ferociously protective of their respective territories, but helpful toward those who treated the literature and librarians well. They helped new scribes navigate the stacks, alerted the librarians to any works that were in need of repair, and punished those who didn't behave. They took on the characteristics of their territory, of course. The keeper of mathematics had skin made of etched clay and spoke in statements. The keeper of plays liked to wear masks and use props. The keeper of philosophy wore a mirror face. They did have a sense of humor.

But the country was invaded and many cities burned. The capital was set aflame, too, and so was its library. All except for one small part.

∻

Pinax fell quiet.

"Except for which part?" Augusta asked.

"I do love these," Pinax mumbled, and picked up a crumbly yellow cake from the tray.

"What does any of this have to do with anything?" Augusta said.

"It's my story," Pinax said. "I am the keeper of the registry. And my story is important to yours."

"So explain it to me," Augusta said.

Pinax smiled at her. "Perhaps if we were friends, I might. But so far I don't know that I trust you."

"But we are friends." Augusta gestured at the table. "I brought you cake, you made tea, we are having it together."

"You're only interested in what I can do for you," Pinax said.

"Yes," Augusta replied. "That's why you're my friend, because you can do something for me. You can help me find Phantasos, so I can go home."

Pinax raised an eyebrow. "That is not how friendship works."

"Then how does it work?" said Augusta in exasperation.

"Friendship," Pinax said, "is not an exchange of gifts. Friendship is built on trust. I don't know if you are trustworthy, Augusta. I don't know that I can trust you with the information you seek. You are uncultured and rude. But I see potential in you. And that potential person might be a friend of mine."

Augusta scoffed. "I am not uncultured and rude. I am a lady."

"Perhaps in your world and your time. But I need to see that you have some sort of conscience," Pinax said. "That you will use the information I have wisely."

"But I am wise," Augusta said. "I'm clever."

Pinax sighed. "Let's call it a mentorship for now. I will teach you things."

"If I learn things, will you tell me where to find Phantasos?"
"Perhaps. Come back tomorrow and we will talk more."

Augusta returned home only to realize that she had no maid. She wandered down the street until she spotted a young man who looked appropriate. He followed without protest, although he kept asking questions. Who was Augusta? Where were they going? What was he supposed to do? He became more pliable after a beating. Augusta settled in her room to wait. She would have to have patience until Pinax gave her the information she needed.

11

"Trees!" Thistle said weakly, and pointed at the horizon, where shapes rose like slender fingers against the sky.

He was beginning to weigh on Dora's back now. Her feet were heavy, and her arms were tired from holding on to Thistle's legs. Still, she would not put him down. He was more tired than she was.

The tall grass gave way to dusty gravel. Ahead lay a stone city, its border guarded by enormous, forbidding statues. A naked woman with wings and bird feet held a sharp-looking hook in her hand. A cloaked figure rested its bony hand on a scythe. A man with a canine head held a staff and a looped cross. A twisted old woman in robes brandished a long knife. As Dora walked in among them, the statues seemed to stare at her, although not in a hostile way; it was more as if she were being studied and measured.

A road flanked by those tall trees led through the metropolis. The stone buildings on either side were in a jumble of wildly

different styles: pyramids, columned temples, ornate tents, simple slabs leaned against one another. Eventually, they came to an
open space, a square intersected by a wide canal with an arched
bridge. Thistle climbed down from Dora's back.

On the other side of the canal stood a house unlike the others.
It was made of wood, with a pointed metal-tiled roof and stained-
glass windows, and it sat on three pairs of large spoked wheels.
It looked like a carriage of some sort, if a carriage could also be
a house. Dora could hear the drone of voices and snatches of
music. She walked across the bridge. Thistle followed in her wake.

Thistle peeked in through the nearest arched window, which
sat just low enough that he could reach it. The light from the
inside cast his face in jewel tones. Dora looked over his shoulder. The room was unfurnished; the floor planks were naked. The
light came from a huge chandelier that hung from the ceiling,
set with scores of candles. Nothing moved in there, but still the
noise from something like a party bled outside. A multitude of
voices, the clink of glass, a melody played on strings. Dora circled
the structure. The long wall on the other side was set with wide
stairs that almost, but not quite, touched the ground. It did not,
however, have a door. Just more windows. Dora climbed the stairs
and looked inside. The room looked empty, just like it had from
the other side. She heard Thistle rapping on the glass. The noise
remained unchanged.

"No door?" Thistle said as he came around the corner.

"No door," Dora replied.

"Should we break in?" Thistle asked.

The sound of shrill pipes in the distance interrupted Dora
before she could reply.

·:·

A small procession came walking up the road to the square and stopped on the middle of the bridge. Two people draped in white carried a bier, on which rested a human form under a sheet. The tan young man who carried the back end had curly brown hair and a square face; the girl at the front was rosy and wiry, her dark blond hair in a simple twist slung across her shoulder. At the head of the procession walked an older woman, stout and powerful but bent in sorrow. She wore layers of white linen, brilliant against her brown skin. A crown of twigs sat atop her braided black hair. She was playing a double-piped flute, an insistent and weeping melody that harmonized with itself in chords that made Dora clap her hands over her ears.

The pallbearers set the bier down on the ground. The older woman lowered her flute. Then they all stared at Dora and Thistle as one. When the older woman spoke, her voice was deep and sonorous.

"Who disturbs our rites?"

"Hello," Dora said.

Thistle bowed. "Madam, I am called Thistle, and my companion Dora."

Dora didn't bow. "Who are you? Who is the dead person?" she said.

The girl peeled the sheet back. The man on the bier was dressed in an oilcloth jacket over a gray knitted sweater. He wore a cap that obscured his eyes, but his cheeks were coarse and weather-beaten.

Dora pointed. "Who is that?"

Thistle pinched her arm.

"He was a fisherman," the crowned woman intoned. "A simple man, a god-fearing man."

"He was Knut Olesen of Lillesand," the young man filled in. "The first victim of a great invasion."

"He had made the best catch in a decade when they killed him," said the girl. "He was forty-three years old."

The older woman gestured at the canal. "We come to lay him to rest."

She raised her hands to the sky, as did the young man and the girl.

"Gods of death, hear me," she said. "We consign this man to you."

The young man bent down and picked up the back of the bier. The corpse slid into the water without leaving so much as a ripple.

"So ends Knut Olesen's story," the woman said.

"So ends the story," the others said in unison.

They stood with their heads bowed for a moment. Then, improbably, the girl broke into a grin. The older woman nodded and smiled.

"Well done," she said to the others.

There was a splash from the canal.

"Well, that was wet," a voice said.

An old man rose out of the water and climbed onto the cobblestones. He looked nothing like Knut Olesen the fisherman, but he was wearing the same clothes, now soaked. His face was alive and draped in kindly folds. He walked onto the bridge and joined hands with the tall woman. The pallbearers joined them on either side. They bowed as one.

"You have seen The First Victim!" the crowned woman said. "I present to you, in order of appearance: our beloved Nestor, as Knut Olesen!"

The old man stepped forward, flinging his arms out like a dancer.

"Journeyman, as Pallbearer One!"

The young man bowed solemnly.

"Apprentice, as Pallbearer Two!"

The girl bobbed a quick curtsy.

"And finally"—the woman herself stepped up—"the High Priestess, played by yours truly. I am Director, and I hope you have enjoyed our show, whoever you are and wherever you may be."

Dora had a sudden urge to clap her hands. She did. The people on the bridge looked down at them.

"It's an actual audience," Apprentice said.

"Yes, it is," Director said. "Who are you?"

"We already told you," Dora replied.

"You told the Priestess and her aides. You didn't tell us."

"I'm Dora. He's Thistle."

"I apologize, madam," Thistle said. "She is very direct."

"Oh, that's okay." Director shrugged. "We're not exactly people with manners."

She looked Thistle up and down, and then Dora. "How did you get here?"

"We walked," Dora replied.

"I see. From where?"

"The other side of the lake. And the crossroads."

Director nodded. "And your purpose?"

"We're looking for someone," Dora said.

"Who?"

"A theater troupe. Ghorbi said we'd know them when we saw them," Thistle said.

"Ghorbi," Nestor muttered.

Director arched an eyebrow. "I see. Then allow me to really introduce us." She threw her arms out. "We are the Memory Theater."

Behind her, the others bowed again.

"We play stories so that they may be remembered," Director

continued. "We play true stories. We write them into the book of the universe, if you will, or weave them into the tapestry, if that sounds better. When we do that, the event will live on. It is recorded and will always have happened. Like here: Knut Olesen's death, recorded."

"But we usually don't have an audience," Journeyman said.

"A visible audience," said Nestor, and scowled at him. "The universe is watching."

"So this is quite an occasion," Director finished.

There was a short moment of silence in which the troupe and the siblings looked at each other. Dora's stomach rumbled.

"I'm hungry," Dora said. "Do you have food?"

Director broke into a smile. "Of course we do! To the wagon."

The troupe marched over to the mysterious house on wheels. They walked up the stairs, and Journeyman fiddled with the center window. Somehow he unhooked it, then pushed. The whole wall to the right of the window folded and slid aside on rails. Director grabbed the left section and pushed it the other way. What had from the outside looked like an empty space was now a cluttered dressing room, with vanity tables, several stuffed armchairs, and a tiny kitchen with an iron stove next to the open wall. The four actors climbed inside and walked over to the four armoires that covered the back wall, where they unceremoniously stripped naked and changed into blue coveralls. Journeyman was done first and opened a cupboard next to the stove, where he started getting out pots and pans.

"Complimentary dinner for our guests!" Director shouted from where she was buttoning her coveralls.

12

Pinax was always at home when Augusta came to call. They would always let her in.

Pinax's home was meticulously ordered but mutable. They were constantly rearranging the books according to different systems: binding, author, category, first sentence in alphabetical order, last sentence in alphabetical order, longest beginning sentence, authors who knew each other. Augusta watched and ate cakes.

Pinax spoke of cities they had lived in, libraries they had visited, and creatures they had encountered: ulda, jinns, strigoi, bacchantes, wordless creatures at the edge of civilization like Pyret and Mörksuggan. These were fascinating stories, but Pinax still wouldn't talk about Augusta's request to help her find Phantasos. They turned to stories about the current age: kings, queens, countries at war. That the streets were dark at night because flying machines might come to drop bombs. These were all important things Pinax apparently thought Augusta should know.

They lent Augusta a book on etiquette, and she read it with some difficulty. These were the codes that humans here lived by, and that Pinax for some reason found important. Most of them were random and pointless, with the exception of how to address superiors, of which Augusta approved. The purpose of etiquette was clear: it was about how to flatter people, which in turn would make them well disposed toward you, which meant you could make them do things for you. It was about wheedling. Well, Augusta could wheedle. She tried some of the suggested techniques on Pinax: she complimented them on their immaculate shoes and manicured nails, and asked how their day was. Pinax brightened visibly, which was encouraging. Augusta tried the same on some of the wood-lice people in the street, but they scurried away without reply. Perhaps they were too intimidated; despite her simple attire, Augusta still radiated magnificence.

She stopped asking Pinax to tell the rest of the library story. Instead, she listened to even more stories, lectures on how to engage with people, even how to cook. Augusta engaged with people. She found a building from which, an elderly gentleman told her, trains transported people to faraway places. You bought a slip of paper to travel on them. Augusta didn't have any money. She didn't need it: she enthralled shopkeepers to hand her new clothes. She could have whatever she wanted from the stores. Fashion—except for suits—was horrible, and food everywhere was dull because of this "rationing." Technology was interesting, however: engines, bicycles, cars, electric lights. Augusta especially liked trains, although she had yet to figure out where she would go. Perhaps she would take a train to Phantasos.

At night she went back to her little house, where her servant was waiting by the stove. Augusta asked him about the things she had seen during the day, but the boy was next to useless except when it came to cooking. His face had been printed on a newspaper that the man on the corner sold. He could not be let out of the house again. Augusta killed him and found another.

Pinax smiled more often, made jokes, and explained them when Augusta missed the fine points. It seemed to Augusta that perhaps this was friendship, even though Pinax had yet to give her what she needed.

The weather grew cooler, and the rosehips along Augusta's street ripened into little orange fruits. When Augusta woke one afternoon and beautified herself with the little wax stick, she realized that something was happening to her face. Faint lines radiated from her eyes and spread across her forehead, and shallow grooves ran from her nostrils to the corners of her mouth. She was aging.

She brought Pinax a box of arrak rolls.

"I have waited and waited," Augusta said. "Something is wrong with my face now."

"Yes, you have waited for a month," Pinax replied. "You have been very patient. Come inside."

"Would you like to see it?" they asked as they drank their tea.

"Would I like to see what?" Augusta replied.

"The library."

"We're in it."

"Not this library," Pinax said. "The library from the story."

⊹

Pinax led her into the study next to the sitting room, where they opened a door. Inside, a set of stairs wound down into a dimly lit passage that smelled of smoke. The air was noticeably warmer here. Augusta followed Pinax for what could have been fifty steps or a hundred until they reached a pair of wooden double doors. They swung open on well-oiled hinges, and the heat hit Augusta's face like a wall.

The room might have been ten meters across. Shelves lined the stone walls from top to bottom, crammed with all kinds of writing. There were rolls, codices of bamboo, vellum, and wood, stacks and rows of clay tablets, inscribed bone plates. The air was dry and stank of burning paper. A roar filled the room, the sound of fire raging on the other side of the walls. Augusta heard muffled shouts in some unfamiliar language. She walked along the shelves, trailing her fingers over books and rolls and stacks.

"This is it," Pinax said. "What do you think?"

Augusta plucked a scroll from a pile and examined it. The outside was covered in odd symbols. Pinax pried it out of her hands before she could unroll it, and put it back on the shelf.

"I'm missing something, aren't I," Augusta said.

Pinax made a small sound that Augusta couldn't interpret. Perhaps frustration.

"Let's go back upstairs," they said, "and I will tell you the rest of the story."

The queen had nightmares about fire.

In her dreams, fire ate its way through the library shelf by shelf, section by section. Night after night, she woke up screaming and rushed down to her books only to discover them unharmed, and the little guardians confused that she was in such a state. Her soothsayer interpreted her dreams as merely symbolic. The queen pretended to agree with him but still ordered a new section built into the library: a registry that also held copies of the greatest works in each section. The official purpose was to present the essence of the library. Not long after the new registry was completed, a runner came to inform her that a foreign army had crossed the border to their country.

The nation was old and had not been at war for a long time. It had relied on negotiation and good relations for centuries; its armies were trimmed down to a bare minimum.

We had seen wars before, but never had anyone tried to burn the library. Invaders had understood the value of knowledge. These new enemies had no respect for literature. To them, destroying thousands of years' worth of knowledge was a strategic act. They rushed across the country, leaving burning temples and ruined monuments in their wake.

The queen was inside the library when they came. The soldiers forced the doors open and poured inside. They drenched the shelves in oil and set their torches to them. Fire devoured dry wood and vellum and paper. Keepers screamed in terror as they perished with their works. The queen donned her helmet and spoke to me.

"If anything can be saved, Keeper," she told me, "let it be the knowledge of what was once here. Protect our memory."

Pinax poured themself some more tea. Augusta sat very still.

"Some keepers escaped," they said. "The keeper of plays, for example. They live on. And then there's me."

"You," Augusta said.

"Yes. I was the keeper of the registry. That's what my name means. I took what remained of the library and made a little world to keep it safe. But it is so much work to maintain. What happened to the rest of the library is catching up. So, slowly but surely, the room is getting hotter. The fire outside, the fire in the burning library a long time ago, is trying to get in."

Pinax sipped from their cup. "I don't know if I myself will survive. I am a genius loci; my life is tied to a place. And that place is burning down. I have built new homes in various places over the years and brought the little pocket universe with me. I thought perhaps time and distance would make it easier, that it would somehow weaken the bond between my stolen room and the rest of the library. And so I ended up here, in this cold country."

"You created a world within a world," Augusta said.

Pinax nodded. "I did. It just took words, and will. As the Keeper, I knew every book in the library. I knew the spells and incantations to build and protect such a place." They pointed at her with the cup. "Just like you did, once upon a time."

"I did?"

"Your society did. Phantasos and Mnemosyne sought me out. I lived in Paris in those days, but I was not unknown among those with mystical knowledge. Your colleagues traveled all the way from this town to ask me how to create a world. I taught them."

"Ah," Augusta said.

"You created the Gardens through a mutual agreement that it be separate from Earth," Pinax continued. "It would be perfect, innocent, unravaged by the passage of time, like the Arcadia of myth. When you started asking questions about time, Augusta, you risked the existence of that place. That is why Mnemosyne cast you out."

Augusta felt like her chest was shrinking.

"And it was for the best," Pinax said. "You created a world of your own, and you lost yourselves in it. Phantasos described it to me. He said that you grew senile, then mad. That you forgot who you were and why you had chosen to create the Gardens. He said he was sick of ruling a nation of idiots."

"Where is he?" Augusta asked. "Tell me. Help me find him."

"Phantasos?" Pinax looked at her. "Are you ready for that?"

"Look at me," Augusta said. "It has been a month, and I'm growing old." She drew a finger from her right nostril to the corner of her mouth. "Here. See?"

Pinax's mouth was a line. "There are answers in the library, but you are not ready."

"You promised," Augusta said. "I have done everything you said."

"I promised nothing," Pinax replied. "It has only been a month."

"I'll die of old age before you tell me anything!" Augusta shouted.

There was nothing for it. She stormed out.

That night in a dream, Augusta stood with others in a circle around three divans. They were in the conservatory; moonlight shone down on them through crystal panes. She recognized Euterpe, Walpurgis, Tempestis, Cymbeline, Virgilia, the rest. Their clothes were less elaborate than they should be. Their unpainted faces looked smooth and very young. Augusta's heart swelled to see them. She loved them. It was love.

On the three divans sat the Aunts, hands resting on their thighs. Behind them stood Mnemosyne and a man Augusta didn't recognize. He was slight, with fair hair falling in perfect ringlets around a pointed face. He looked around the circle, and for a moment his eyes bored into Augusta's.

Mnemosyne and the man joined hands, and the lords and

ladies in the circle began to chant, long words with soft consonants and open vowels. This is our land, the words meant. Our pure
and innocent land. Time is no more. Only this blessed night, in Arcadia,
forever.

The chant ended. The Aunts lay down as one. A shudder went
through the air.

"Time," Mnemosyne said into the silence, "has stopped. We
are free. Let us cast off our old lives. Let us forget the old world
and be innocent."

Then they were in the statuary grove, dancing to a slow and
uneven rhythm. Mnemosyne and the man sat on a dais before
them, watching.

Augusta sat in her bower. A servant put makeup on her face.
They smiled at each other. The brush was cold against her lips.
She was bored. The servant's skin was smooth. Why should
not the servants be adorned? Let us paint the servants. Flowers
for their names.

They danced in the statuary grove, but it was like moving
through muddy water. The wine tasted sour.

A croquet game on the grand lawn. Someone fell. Breaking
glass. Blood spilled down a servant's shirt. The arterial red cut
through the dullness like a shout. Such a pretty shade. Why
should not the servants bleed? Flowers for their names.

They danced in the statuary grove. The man stood up and left
the dais.

They danced in the statuary grove.
They danced in the statuary grove.
They danced in the statuary grove.

13

"So," Nestor said, "it's time you explain why you searched us out."

Thistle and Dora sat with Director and Nestor on the stairs to the house on wheels. Apprentice was clearing the dirty dishes away, and Journeyman was organizing costumes in the armoires. Director and Nestor shared a hookah, making watery burbles and puffs of cherry-scented smoke. They had all been noisy for a long time now. They were talking back and forth, quick and chittering like birds. The babble closed over Dora's head like water, pressed at her from all sides. It was getting very hard to keep up, but Thistle did the talking and replied to Nestor's question.

"We're looking for someone called Augusta Prima," he said.

"And from where does this Augusta Prima hail?" Director asked.

"The Gardens," Thistle said.

"Which gardens?"

"That's what they're called," Thistle said. "The Gardens."

Dora made an effort to jump in. "There's an orchard and a conservatory and a statue forest and a croquet lawn," she said. "But no time."

The others looked up when she spoke.

Nestor raised an eyebrow and blew a smoke ring. "No time, eh. I recognize that."

"We've played it," Director said. "*The Creation of Arcadia.*"

"That's right." Nestor nodded. "I believe Apprentice was new at the time."

"I know it!" Apprentice came over and sat down. "I played . . . I can't recall who I played. I was so nervous. What happened after they made the place?"

"Bad things," Thistle said.

"They went insane, didn't they," Director said. "It was such an audacious idea."

"What else do you know?" Thistle asked.

Nestor shook his head. "That's it," he said. "That's what we know."

Director held up a book that had been resting on the step next to her. The cover was marbled and had an ornate spine.

"This is the playbook," she said. "That's where we find the manuscripts. A new one appears, and we're off. We don't know anything else but what it says on the page."

"Like this time it was about that fisherman," Apprentice said. "Knut. He was fishing when the army came. But that's all we know."

"We do know that it took place on Earth," Nestor said. "But not much else. We came here to the city of the dead to enact his burial."

"The city of the dead," Dora said.

Director nodded. "We come here quite often. Births and deaths are popular with the book."

"Ghorbi said so," Thistle said.

Again, Nestor muttered something to himself. Then he said, "Now, what is your quest?"

"Augusta has my name. I need it back, so I can find my way home to my parents."

"And you, Dora?"

Dora reached down and put an arm around Thistle, who leaned back against her. "I go where he goes," she said.

Director hummed.

Journeyman watched them from a stool, where he sat mending a robe. Every time Dora looked at him, he was watching her. Apprentice had cleared away the dishes and came over to sit with them.

"Ghorbi sent you?" Apprentice asked.

"She helped us," Thistle said. "And said you could help us find Augusta."

Nestor made a sour face. "Calling in her favor. Couldn't even come by herself."

"You know her?" Dora asked.

Nestor glared at the hookah. Director patted him on the shoulder.

"Ghorbi and Nestor have history," she said. "She saved him from a great library when it burned. It was long ago, before the rest of us came along. Of course she wouldn't come personally, Nestor. You would have made a scene."

The talk became a cloud again. It pressed in on Dora's head from all directions. Everything was too loud, too sharp.

"Thistle," she whispered. "It's too much."

Thistle looked up at her. "I'm sorry, Dora. I should have noticed that you were tired."

He stood up and took Dora's hand. "Dora needs to rest. Is there somewhere quiet she can go?"

"Was it something we said?" Nestor asked.

"She just needs to be alone," Thistle said.

"The trapdoor?" Journeyman said from his stool.

He beckoned Thistle and Dora over to the back of the wagon and lifted a hatch in the floor. A ladder led down into a small space where Dora could glimpse pillows and blankets.

"There's a mattress and everything. I go there for naps."

Dora climbed down the steps and made a nest.

"Will you be all right?" Thistle asked from above.

"Close the door," Dora said.

She could hear and see nothing. She could breathe again in this quiet place.

Dora woke to swaying movement. Thistle was next to her, drawing quiet sleep-breaths. The air was stuffy. Dora climbed up the ladder and opened the hatch.

The wall of the house was back up. Faint light shone in through the windows, moving, as if they were traveling through a forest or under water. The troupe members were sitting in armchairs around something on the floor. They were dressed in bathrobes, talking in rapid voices. As Dora came closer, she saw that the thing on the floor was a map, except it wasn't. The sheet of paper on the floor had coastlines and places marked out, but over it sat something that looked like a canopy made of thick metal wire. From the canopy hung paper silhouettes and glass spheres at different heights, all of them connected to one another and the map with thread.

Apprentice spotted Dora and waved at her. "Breakfast?"

Dora nodded. Apprentice guided her to an armchair and handed her a deep bowl filled with some sort of stew.

"Sorry," she said. "We're between worlds. No exciting food."

The stew was lukewarm and tasted like nothing much, which was nice. "Thank you," Dora said.

Nestor smiled at her. "You've been down there for a while. I hope you feel better."

Dora pointed at the canopy on the floor. "What's that?"

"It's a map," Apprentice said behind her.

"A very imperfect one," Nestor added. "You see, it only describes four dimensions, and badly at that."

He pointed at a miniature carriage suspended on a silver thread in the middle of the structure. It was moving on a very slow downward trajectory. "Right now we are somewhere around here, in transit between worlds." Then he pointed at a place on the paper map on the floor. "But 'there,' for example, is relative. These places are not stationary. They are like floating islands."

"You could consider the universe an ocean," Director said, "and us a ship."

"Can you go everywhere?" Dora asked.

"In theory," Director replied. "We go wherever the playbook leads us. Most of the time it's about reenacting an important scene that needs remembering. Sometimes we pay tribute to important people. Sometimes to ordinary people, like Knut Olesen the fisherman. We stay backstage, though. We see and experience, but we don't touch."

"I've never been frontstage," Apprentice said bitterly.

"That's not your job," Director said, and it seemed that they had had this conversation many times before.

The whole thing made Dora's head hurt. "It's too much," she said.

"Thistle tells us you're different," Nestor said, "and we should try not to jabber too much at you."

"What are you?" Apprentice asked. "You're not human."

"I don't know," Dora said. "Ghorbi says I was grown like a root."

Nestor drew the corners of his mouth down. "Yes. Thistle told us she . . . traded you, like cattle. How could you trust her after what she did to you?"

"She said she was sorry. She took us out of there."

Nestor rolled his eyes and turned to Director. "Did you hear that? Ghorbi says she's sorry."

"Oh, come," Director said. "She has a profession like the rest of us. She broke your heart, we know."

"Well, I'm not the forgiving type," Nestor replied.

"There's nothing to forgive. You're being unreasonable. And she did do you a favor."

Nestor scowled. "You wouldn't understand. You've never been in love."

"I have too," Director snapped. "But I have never demanded that anyone love me back."

Dora looked down at her bowl. She had emptied it without noticing.

"Dora," Journeyman said next to her. "Would you like more?"

Dora nodded, and Journeyman filled her bowl again. The others returned to the map, but Nestor kept his frown.

Dora finished the stew. When next she looked up, the doors were pushed aside and light streamed in. The troupe was gathered in a little clearing: Apprentice lay on the ground with her legs in the air, Journeyman resting on the soles of Apprentice's feet, their hands linked to keep balance. Director and Nestor juggled little balls back and forth, calling out words Dora didn't understand. Thistle sat with his back against a tree next to the carriage. He was dressed in a pair of the company's coveralls; they were a little too big for him. He looked relaxed, but his sleeves were rolled down and fastened tightly around his wrists. His face was all stubbly now, and his russet hair curled in a halo around his head. He smiled at Dora as she sat down next to him, and brushed at her skirts with his hand.

"You could use some clean clothes, Dora," he said. "And a bath."

Dora considered this for a moment. "Yes."

There was a little pond among the trees, its water coppery but clear. Dora dived in and swam along the bottom, where crayfish crawled in under rocks and perch darted away from her. Something bigger lurked in the forest of water lily stalks but retreated as she came closer. The sun shot rays of liquid light through the water. Down here there was only the sound of the pulse in her ears and the small noises of water life. Dora only came up because her lungs were burning. Thistle was standing on the shore, a towel in his hand.

"I'm not done," Dora told him.

Thistle smiled and put the towel down on a rock.

Dora dived back down under the surface. She counted crayfish and stalked the huge thing among the water lilies, caught a little perch and petted it, chased water striders, and tasted the sedge that grew on the shore. She got out of the water only when the sun sank so low it was difficult to see.

She came back to the camp dressed in a pair of coveralls that someone had left at the water's edge. The legs and sleeves were too short. There had been a pair of boots, too, and she carried them under her arm. The others had made a fire in front of the carriage and moved the armchairs and sofa onto the grass. A big trumpet flower made of metal was playing tinny-sounding music. The smell of baking bread and some other food hung in the air. Thistle sat in one of the armchairs, leaning back, arms and legs relaxed. When he saw Dora, he smiled. The circle of people opened and let her in.

"Excellent," Director said as Dora sat down on the grass next to Thistle. "Sorry about the sizing. They were the biggest coveralls we could find." She pointed at Dora's feet. "What about the boots?"

Dora shook her head. "I don't like shoes."

"Fair enough." Director held out a bowl. "Soup?"

They ate and talked and the music played. It was easier to be in the crowd after playing in the quiet water. The troupe told stories about worlds they had visited, plays they had staged. Thistle spoke quietly about things in the Gardens. The last light in the sky died, and Journeyman and Apprentice cleared the dishes away.

Nestor stood and stretched. "I believe it's time."

"Time for what?" Dora said.

Director grinned and held up the red playbook. "Your play appeared!"

14

Instead of ringing the bell by Pinax's door, Augusta fed roses into the mailbox, one by one. They crunched and tore as she pushed them in, releasing the heavy scent of late summer. The door abruptly opened.

"You can stop doing that."

Pinax stood over her. Their eyebrows were knotted. They looked decidedly unhappy.

"It is a gift," Augusta said. "I thought you might like roses."

"You had best come in," Pinax said.

Someone else was already sitting in one of the armchairs in the library: a very tall woman in dark robes, a scarf like shadow draped over her hair. Her long features were familiar, her yellow eyes. As Augusta entered the room, the woman rose from her chair, and it seemed she almost touched the ceiling.

"Augusta," she said, and her voice was low and sweet. "Fancy that."

"I believe you and Ghorbi have met," Pinax said behind her.

"You," Augusta blurted. "You!"

Ghorbi smiled. Her teeth looked uncomfortably sharp. Augusta's face felt numb and cold, then suddenly became hot as rage overtook her.

"You had me cast out!" she screamed. "It's all your fault! Do you have any idea what I've been through?"

"You asked me a question," Ghorbi said. "I gave you the knowledge for free.

"I was just about to leave," she continued, and turned to Pinax. "I hope you're happy with the package, librarian."

"Extremely," Pinax replied. "Thank you, my friend."

"You can't go," Augusta said. "I won't let you. You're going to get me back in. You owe me."

Ghorbi took a step toward Augusta and stared down at her. "Owe you?" she said, in that same soft voice. "I did you a favor. You will pay it back, in time. Although perhaps not to me."

Augusta took a step backward and collided with a bookshelf.

Ghorbi straightened. "Goodbye, Augusta Prima. Goodbye, my dear Pinax."

She swept out of the room. A moment later, the front door closed with a click.

"Don't go!" Augusta shouted, and rushed down the hallway. The door had locked itself. When she managed to get it open, the street was empty.

"Come back!" she yelled, and the echo of her voice bounced against the buildings.

"Ghorbi is an old friend." Pinax stood behind her in the hallway with that same expression they had worn when they first let her in.

"She told me all of it," they continued. "It's worse than I could ever have imagined. I don't know how you could do those things."

"Things?" Augusta repeated.

"You never told me there were children. Phantasos never told me." Pinax's voice trembled. "The things you did to them. You lured them into your world, abused them, stole their whole lives. As if they weren't people."

"They *aren't* people," Augusta retorted. When she saw Pinax's face, she realized that this was entirely the wrong thing to say.

"I let you into my house," Pinax said. "I thought, Here is a lost soul I might save. I thought I could rehabilitate you. But I see now that you are a lost cause. You are a monster."

"I am not! I can be good."

"When?" Pinax asked. "When were you good? When were you kind?"

Their expression was unreadable. Augusta felt a pit open in her stomach. "You hate me," she said.

Pinax pointed at the door. "Leave. You are not welcome in my house anymore."

When she got home, Augusta's current servant was huddled next to the stove. Augusta strangled him. She didn't bother to drag him into the chamber; it was full. The house had begun to smell. Standing over the boy's corpse, Augusta considered what to do. There was nothing for her here except the information Pinax guarded.

Pinax would not welcome her. They had called her a monster. It was nonsense. She only did what was necessary. And now she would have to do it again. Pinax had rejected her—rejected her!—

but she could take the information she wanted. It was only a matter of waiting until nightfall.

Augusta walked through the streets one last time. The night was absolute; everyone had covered their windows, waiting for the enemy to rain fire on the city.

The stone house was a hard shape against the streak of stars. Nothing moved in the street. Augusta stood back and considered the windows on the bottom floor. There, to the far right, should be the room where she and Pinax had taken their tea. Next to it, the kitchen. The mullioned window sat just about low enough that she could climb inside. Augusta picked up one of the rocks that edged the flower bed in front of the house. The bottom right pane shattered with a brittle noise, and Augusta paused. The street was still quiet. No sound came from inside the house. Augusta carefully reached in and undid the latch on the inside. She scratched her hand on the shards that remained in the frame, but not too badly. The window swung outward, and Augusta lifted the blackout curtain to crawl inside.

She fumbled her way along the wall. Across from the kitchen, the closed door to what must be Pinax's bedroom; she shuffled along and found the second door to the left that led to the study. She put her ear to the door. It was quiet. She scratched on the wood with her fingers. When there was no reply, she pushed down the handle and peeked inside. Nothing. She felt the wall next to the door and found the light switch. The study was very orderly, just like everything else in this house: bookshelves, a large desk, a chair, and a lamp. At the back of the room, the door that led to the hidden library. She tried the handle. It was unlocked.

A wave of heat hit Augusta's face as she descended the spiral staircase, and she could hear the distant roar of flames. The double doors were ajar.

The room was illuminated by some light source that Augusta couldn't make out; shadows danced across the books and scrolls on the shelves. Pinax sat cross-legged on the floor with their back turned. They didn't move as Augusta took the last few steps inside and stepped around them.

Pinax's eyes were closed; they were seemingly lost in meditation or sleep.

"Pinax," Augusta whispered, but the librarian didn't react.

Augusta turned her attention to the shelves.

At the very edge of a shelf, almost hidden beneath a scroll, she saw a flat lacquered box, unmarked. It was the only thing in here that was not ancient. Augusta tucked the box under her arm and backed out of the room. Pinax remained where they were.

Back in the study, Augusta closed the door behind her and opened the box. It was full of envelopes, all with Pinax's name on the back, some of them with addresses: Vienna, Cairo, Paris. She opened some of them. They were in all kinds of languages, most of which she could not read. Then, there was a cream-colored envelope in thick paper addressed in Latin: To my dear friend Pinax. Augusta opened it.

The letter was short.

I will go north, to Frostviken. Thank you for your kind hospitality. Wish me well. We will not meet again.

—P

÷

There was a northbound train in the morning. Augusta watched people climb aboard. Then she herself mounted the steps and claimed a compartment. The train conductor didn't trouble her after she had spoken to him firmly. The train chugged northward, and the landscape gradually changed from farmland to snow-flecked blunt mountains.

15

"Our play?" Thistle said.

"The two of you have told us your stories, so we must play them," Director said.

The company turned the sofa to face the carriage, folded back the wall of the house, and climbed inside. Dora and Thistle sat down on the sofa. Thistle took Dora's hand. A velvet curtain unfurled from the ceiling and covered the house's interior.

A gong rang, and the curtain rose. The armoires, the kitchen, the mess had disappeared; instead there was a luscious grove with marble statues peeking out from behind leafy trees. The backdrop was the turquoise of just after sunset. Little lanterns hung in the branches of the trees.

Nestor stood at the far edge of the stage, dressed in a doublet and puffy knee pants.

"Welcome, all, to the mystic Gardens," he intoned, "a timeless place of magic and debauchery, ruled by mad and fickle lords and ladies. Here is a boy, lured away from his parents. Little does he know what fate will befall him."

Apprentice wandered onstage as a boy. He was dressed in simple trousers and a shirt with a rounded collar, his hair smoothed back into a queue. He looked around the grove with wide eyes.

"I thought I saw a light," he said. "I thought I heard a song. It was so beautiful, I had to follow. Now all is quiet. Where did it go?"

"Oh, it is all here," said a voice from the other side of the stage.

Director emerged from the right, dressed in a brocade coat and a shirt with lace ruffles. Thistle gasped. Director looked thinner, her features sharper, and her kohl-rimmed eyes had a predator's unblinking stare. She stalked across the stage like a wild beast. She looked very much like Augusta.

"Who have we here?" she said to the boy, who stared at her in awe. "All alone in the woods."

"What is this marvelous place?" the boy asked.

Augusta made a sweeping gesture. "These are the Gardens, where youth and beauty celebrate a bright summer night. Will you join us in the revels?"

"Oh, I don't know," the boy said. "But I am awfully hungry."

Augusta waved her left hand and seemed to conjure an apple out of thin air. "Here, my dear. Taste this."

The boy took the apple.

Thistle tensed up on the sofa. "Don't eat it," he mumbled.

Dora put a hand on his knee. "It's only pretend," she said.

Thistle let out a groan as the boy bit into the apple, chewed, and swallowed.

"I have never tasted anything sweeter," the boy said.

"Nor will you ever again," Augusta replied, "for the fruit of the Gardens is legendary. Now tell me your name."

The boy stood on his toes and whispered something into Augusta's ear.

"Very good, my darling," Augusta said, and took his hand.

The boy smiled up at her.

"I have your name, and you have eaten of our fruit," Augusta said. "I name you Thistle, and a thistle you shall become."

The curtain fell. On the sofa, Thistle curled up against Dora.

"Scene two!" Nestor announced.

The curtain rose again, and the backdrop had changed: a vast horizon of undulating mountains, their tops scraped soft and covered in snow. In the middle of the stage lay a pile of dirt.

Director swept in from stage right. Somehow she had managed to change into another costume in a matter of seconds: she was wrapped in black silk that fluttered around her as she moved. Her eyes shone a startling yellow.

"How do they do that?" Thistle whispered.

Director shaded her eyes and spied across the stage.

"Where is the seed that I sowed? Deep did I plant it, in the heart of this ancient mountain range. Long have I waited for it to take root. I, Ghorbi, am patient, but my patience has limits."

The pile of dirt moved.

"Aha!" Ghorbi cried, and hurried over.

A hand reached out of the pile and waved in the air. Ghorbi took it. Journeyman, dressed in a grubby shift, emerged from the mound and stood up.

"There she is," Ghorbi announced. "The daughter of the mountain, big and strong."

It did look very much like Dora, wearing what must have been a wig, although so well made that it looked like real hair. Journeyman-as-Dora's form was rounded and powerful, and she stood with both feet firmly planted on the ground. She gazed out at the audience, not seeming to notice them. Then she looked at Ghorbi.

"What is my name?" Dora asked on the stage, her voice soft but strong.

"Your name is your own," Ghorbi said. "But I will lend you one, if you like: Dora."

"Scene three!" Nestor announced. "Thistle and Dora."

Onstage, Dora sat in the shade of a tree whose branches drooped with apples. Her eyes were vacant, and she was covered in dirt. She was humming tunelessly to herself. Then, from the left, Thistle walked in. His shirt and hands were spattered scarlet. Behind him, Director was Augusta again, pushing him ahead of her into the orchard.

"There," she announced. "Here is your charge. When you are not with me, you will mind the giant and make sure she makes no trouble. If she does, you will be sorry." She took a step backward and disappeared.

Dora looked up at Thistle and got to her feet.

"You are hurt," she said.

"I am indeed," Thistle said, but stood up straight.

"Who are you?" Dora asked. "Why are you bleeding?"

"They call me Thistle, and this is what they do to all us servants. What do they call you?"

"Dora. I know not where I am, and my father won't speak to me."

Thistle nodded and took Dora's hand. "I have been sent to

teach you the ways of the Gardens. I will teach you how to speak, and where to hide from our masters."

Dora looked down at him. "Will you be my brother, then?"

"I will," Thistle answered.

"Then I will protect you," Dora said, "as well as I can."

They embraced, and the curtain fell.

When the curtain rose again, Journeyman-Dora and Apprentice-Thistle stood center stage, holding hands. They didn't look much like Dora or Thistle anymore, just actors dressed in costumes. On either side, Director and Nestor threw kisses at Dora and Thistle. Journeyman's face was expressionless; Apprentice's eyes were brimming.

The company bowed and thanked their visible and invisible audience. They cleaned up the stage and themselves, then crowded around the sofa in front of the stage. They looked worn out.

Journeyman walked over to where Dora sat. His eyes were damp. "Can I have a hug?"

Dora let go of Thistle and stood up. Journeyman wrapped his arms around her. He smelled of greasepaint and musk and fresh sweat. He sniffled and drew a shuddering breath against her shoulder. Dora gently patted his back.

Journeyman eventually let go.

"I'm sorry," he said, and dried his eyes on his sleeves. "I get emotional. Playing you was . . . you seem so calm, but your feelings are . . . these huge, slow waves. I was too small for them. You're magnificent."

He gave her another quick hug and a smile, and sat down in a chair. Dora stood where she was, stunned.

"We call it 'bleed,'" Director said. "A strong character—or a strong story—can bleed into your own emotions. This isn't acting, love. We *become* the characters. We *become* the story. Journeyman *was* you. And apparently that was quite a ride."

Apprentice was standing behind the sofa, uncharacteristically quiet, hands on Thistle's shoulders. Her eyebrows were knotted, her jaws working.

"And it looks like Apprentice is bleeding a little as well," Director said, "no pun intended. They're young. It gets easier when you've done this for a while."

"Thank you for letting us play your past," Nestor said. "It was a nice change from all the epic stories that we usually have to stage."

"Indeed," Director said. "You are a part of the tapestry now."

16

Thistle fell asleep on the sofa. Dora went back down to the pond. Little creatures rustled in the grass. She crouched on the beach, stirring her fingers in the water. The sound of footsteps made her turn around. She recognized Journeyman's scent. He crouched down next to her.

"Before I played you, I thought you were just slow."

Dora waited.

Journeyman dipped a hand in the water. "I didn't understand that with slowness comes clarity. That you see everything more clearly, feel more keenly than any of us. When I sat there under the tree . . . I have never felt peace like that. And when the others came onstage, it was like an explosion. I wanted to scream, *I'm not done! Let me be!* I don't know how you can stand it."

Dora looked at her fingers in the water.

"And now I did it to you," Journeyman said. "Talked your head off. I'm sorry."

Dora looked up. Two glowing orbs hung in the sky. Journeyman had changed position.

"I learned," Dora said. "How to move fast. I just need to slow down sometimes."

Journeyman's hand was on her left forearm. His fingers ran up and down her skin in a way that made something shift in her belly.

"You're beautiful," he said.

His scent had changed.

"Is Journeyman your own name?" she asked him.

"I gave mine up," he replied.

Dora took his hand and raised it to her face. Little hairs on his wrist tickled her nose. She felt the thin skin on the inside with her lips. He gasped. She ran her hand in under the sleeve on his shirt and touched the crook of his arm, brushed her fingers over a little mole there. His smell, the sound of his uneven breaths, the skin under her hand. It seemed to flicker somehow, as if he wasn't set in his form.

"Is this your own shape?" she asked.

"It was, to begin with." Journeyman let out a long breath.

His face became a blur, like a picture overlaying another, and another, and another: thin shapes, thick shapes, rugged, soft, masculine, feminine, androgynous, altogether alien. The only firm points were his irises, deep brown and constant. When he spoke, it was with a choir of voices.

"I am more shapes than you can imagine."

He solidified into the youth he had been before.

"Do you like it? This self?" he said with the clear baritone he had used before.

Dora nodded.

Journeyman slipped a hand around her waist.

Dora removed his hand. "No. I need to be alone now."

Journeyman drew back. "Of course. I'm sorry."

When his steps had receded, Dora lay on her back by the pool and stared up at the stars. She walked through the memory of him moment by moment—sight, touch, smell, sound—until she could rest in them. He had no form, yet a form: warm, musky. He had wants. And he wanted her but demanded nothing. Dora could rest in that, too.

17

The station consisted of a short platform and a tiny wooden station building with a sign that read FROSTVIKEN. It lay in a shallow bowl, a bog surrounded by mountains. Augusta had been on the train for a long time; dawn lit the sky from below. The cold air carried a smell of herbs and wet grass. Augusta was the only one to disembark. A sharp whistle blew, and the train trundled off into the distance.

A dirt road ran from the station building and out onto the bog. Augusta walked down the road. Before long, it ended in front of an abandoned house whose roof had fallen in. There was nothing for it but to go out into the wilderness. So, she was here. Phantasos had come here. She would find him and learn his secrets.

"Phantasos!" she yelled into the air. "I have come for you."

She walked across the bog calling his name, shivering in the damp cold.

The sun rose and drowned the world in golden light. The

bog was vast, dotted by twisted birch trees. White-tipped grass edged the pools. Here and there, little plants bore flame-colored berries that tasted spicy and sour-sweet. Augusta's shoes were soaked through from slipping into the wet hollows that opened up where the ground had seemed solid. She could no longer feel her toes. As the morning passed, stinging insects woke up: little gnats, larger flying things, and a huge fly that stuck itself to her hand and which she had to scrape off. It was maddening. Augusta trudged on toward the nearest mountain, but it didn't seem to come any closer. It must be enormous.

"Phantasos!" Augusta cried out again and again. "Lord of the Gardens! I call you by your name. Show yourself."

It was midday, and still chilly, when Augusta spotted the old man. He was dressed in rubber boots and trousers and a warm-looking brown sweater, and carried a bucket. He leisurely made his way across the bog, avoiding the larger pools. He halted when he saw her and tilted his head. Then he headed her way, stopping here and there to pick something from the ground. Only when he came close did he straighten and look at Augusta. He was wiry, his blue eyes cold in a face sunburned many times over.

"Greetings, old man," Augusta said.

The man studied her for a long moment.

"I thought I heard a voice," he said. Then he looked her over. "What are you doing out here? Are you lost?"

"Perhaps," Augusta said, then used her lady voice. "Say, old man, that's a nice pair of boots and sweater. You should give them to me."

He shook his head. "No."

Resistance. Odd. "Give them to me," Augusta repeated. "I'm cold."

"No wonder. You're wet and that suit of yours isn't any good here."

Augusta decided to try etiquette. "Help me, then," she said.

The old man studied her for a long moment. "Who are you?"

"I'm a traveler," Augusta said. "Just a traveler. From very far away."

He sucked air in through his teeth. "Very far away," he repeated. "Very well. You may call me Nils Nilsson."

"Nils Nilsson," Augusta said. "Please give me your sweater."

"I need my sweater," Nils said, "but if you follow me, I can find another one for you."

Without another word, he set off along a small path Augusta hadn't seen until now. Augusta walked after him, mystified by his resilience. There was something about this man. But she was cold, and she could deal with him when they arrived wherever he was going.

The farm consisted of a small main building, an outhouse, and a barn, all old but well kept. Augusta was exhausted. They had been walking all morning and Nils had kept veering off into the bog to fill his bucket with orange berries.

"Here we are," Nils said. "Welcome."

The kitchen was small, with a stove and a table with some chairs and a wood-framed bench. Everything was worn but clean.

"Do you live here alone?" Augusta asked.

Nils nodded. "I do now," he said. "My wife has passed, and my sons are watching for Germans at the Norwegian border."

"The war," Augusta said.

"Yes, the war," Nils replied. "Now I'm going to fetch you a

sweater and some socks. Take those shoes off or you'll ruin your feet."

Augusta sat down on the bench and fiddled with the curtain in the window. It was embroidered with flower stems. Outside, an animal made a lowing noise, and she craned her neck to look for it.

"The cows," Nils said from the door to the hallway. "Never mind them."

He put a thick knitted sweater and a pair of socks on the table. "Here," he said. "Put these on."

Nils walked over to the stove, where he filled a pot from a bucket. "We need coffee, I think," he said. "And you can tell me what you're doing here."

"I'm looking for someone," Augusta said warily.

"And who might that be?"

"A man," she replied, "who might help me."

"I see," Nils said, and poured something like seeds into a small grinder.

Nils ground the seeds in silence. When the water came to a boil, he poured the grounds into the pot and stirred it. After a moment, he took the pot off the heat. Eventually he poured the mixture into two cups and brought them to the table.

"It's not real coffee, of course," he said. "It's barley. But it'll do."

The mixture tasted earthy and bland, but it was hot, and Augusta drank it.

"Now," Nils said. "Who are you looking for?"

"Phantasos," Augusta said. "His name is Phantasos."

Nils leaned back and crossed his arms over his chest. There was a glint of something in his eyes. "Phantasos. And who might that be?"

"He was a lord who left my home. He ran away."

Nils unfolded his arms and brought the cup of barley brew to his lips. He took a sip, then said, "And do you think he wants to be found? Considering that he ran away."

"I don't care," Augusta said. "Do you know where he is?"

Nils's gaze was sharp. "What do you want with him?"

"I am . . . lost," Augusta said. "He can show me the way home."

"And if he won't?" Nils asked.

"He has to. It's all I have."

"I had a dream," Nils said. "Someone was calling my name. I woke up, and I was restless. So I walked out onto the bog. And there you were."

Augusta sat motionless.

"You called my name," said the man who looked nothing like a lord, who was old and wrinkled and whose teeth were rotting in his skull.

"Your—?" Augusta managed.

Nils nodded. "Long ago. And your name?"

Augusta hesitated. "If you are who you say you are, you would know me."

"I'd rather hear you say it, architect," Nils said.

"Architect?" Augusta said.

Nils smiled. "Yes. You have no memory of building the conservatory?"

Augusta stared at him.

"Of course you don't," Nils said. "Because you fell. Like the rest of them."

"You're Phantasos," Augusta said numbly.

"Not anymore," Nils replied. "I'm just Nils Nilsson now. And I would like you to finish your coffee and be on your way."

Augusta rose from the bench. "You have to get me back into the Gardens," she said. "You know how to get in."

Nils looked up at her, still in his chair. "Why did you leave?"

"Not by choice," Augusta said. "I learned about time. Mnemos-yne cast me out."

"Then you can't go back," Nils said. "We built that place and agreed to lose time. You broke that pact. Mnemosyne won't let you back in."

"I want to go back," Augusta repeated. "Mnemosyne will for-give me."

"Why?"

"What do you mean, why?"

"Why would you want to go back?" Nils said. "That place is hell. It was good at first. We were timeless, ageless; we devoted ourselves to art and magic. But none of you could handle liv-ing the same day over and over. You became bored, because you forgot your purpose. Then you became cruel, because you were bored. That's why I left. I couldn't stand what you had become. I wanted to live a just life again.

"You were an inventor," he continued. "You created marvelous things out of wood and bone and glass. Now look at you."

"Please," Augusta said. "I want to go home."

"I can't help you," Nils replied. "I live here now. I became Nils Nilsson, and I got myself a family, and I grew old. I'll die here. There's no going back from exile."

Augusta gave him a backhanded slap, and he stood up. He looked at her with something like fear.

"You will take me back," she said.

"I can't," he said.

Augusta gripped him by the throat. Nils's right hand shot out and clawed at her face. Augusta screamed as a finger dug into her eye. She kicked out and crushed his kneecap under her heel, then hooked her ankle behind his leg. Nils let go of Augusta's face and fell down on his back. She landed on his chest and dug her knees into his arms. He was strong, but not as strong as she.

"Take me back!" she shouted.

"Can't," Nils panted.

"I'll kill you," Augusta told him. "I'll kill you now if you don't."

Nils shook his head. "If you take my life, you'll have to live it. You will be Nils Nilsson forever or until one of your own recognizes and names you. And they never will."

Augusta drove her fist into his face.

"I curse you," Nils said between broken teeth.

Augusta hit him again. Again, and again, and again, until his face was a ruin.

When Nils had stopped struggling, Augusta rolled over on her back and breathed for a while. She looked up at the underside of the kitchen table, where insects had bored holes into the wood. She closed her eyes. She just needed to rest for a little bit.

Nils woke up alone in the kitchen. His whole body ached. The chairs were overturned, the two cups shattered on the floor. Why were there two cups? There had been a woman, but she was gone. Had she really been here? He held up his hand to his face. Blood had crusted under its thick fingernails. It felt wrong to have such a hand. It was too big, too worn. He got up from the floor with some effort, and pain shot through his lower back. His body felt unfamiliar somehow, like a new and slightly too big suit. Then Svana and Rosa lowed outside, and he realized that they needed milking.

PART III

MOUNTAINS

18

Journeyman smiled as Dora came down the steps of the carriage. The others sat by a huge fire, wrapped in blankets. She looked at the fur Journeyman offered her. It didn't smell like any animal she had ever seen.

A handful of stars pricked the black sky. They were on a beach, a thin strip of sand lit by a luminous ocean on one side and guarded by gnarled trees on the other. Shapes moved in the water, emerging so briefly that Dora didn't have time to see what they were. She turned back to Journeyman.

"I don't need it," she said.

Thistle was talking to Nestor, who sat in his armchair like an old king on a throne, a thick fur over his shoulders.

"She was thrown out of the Gardens. And I want to find her. Will you help me?" Thistle said.

"That way lies death, boy," Nestor said. "She will overpower you."

"I don't care," Thistle said. "I have to try."

Director and Nestor looked at each other for a long moment. Then Journeyman spoke up.

"Ghorbi called in her favor," he said. "We should help them."

Apprentice raised a hand. "I agree."

Director nodded. "It's your favor to return, Nestor, but I would say this is the right time."

Nestor made a disgruntled noise. "Three against one." He looked at Thistle and Dora. "Fine. It's a consensus. We will help you."

Thistle let out a sigh.

"Now," Director said, "do you have something of hers?"

Thistle shook his head.

"Hmm." Director pursed her lips. "Has she been in contact with you? Mixing bodily fluids? Anything of hers that may have rubbed off on you?"

"Thistle," Dora blurted. "She carved you with her nails."

Thistle's face reddened. He glared at Dora.

Director put a hand on Thistle's shoulder. He stepped out of her reach.

"Please show us," Director said.

"It's private," Thistle said.

"I know," Director said. "But if we can see, we can perhaps find Augusta."

Thistle looked at the people gathered around him. He turned and walked down the beach with stiff steps. Director made to go after him.

Dora stepped in her way. "Leave him alone. He's thinking."

÷

Dora waited until she thought Thistle might have had time to consider things. Then, as Apprentice and Journeyman began preparing dinner, she went looking. She saw a line of footprints and followed them. After a little while, she heard a skipping noise, like pebbles on stone. She walked up a low dune; in the hollow beyond stood the ruins of an amphitheater. Thistle sat cross-legged in the middle, playing with something that looked like old bones. He looked up as Dora approached.

"Do you still want to be alone?" Dora asked.

"No," Thistle said.

Dora sat down next to him. Thistle dropped the bones, leaned his head on her shoulder, and wept. When he was down to only sniffles, Dora wiped his cheeks with her sleeves.

"There," she said. "All better."

Thistle let out a short laugh. "No makeup to smudge anymore."

"I won't let them harm you," Dora said.

"I don't think they would. It's just hard."

"I know." Dora stood and helped Thistle up.

They climbed the amphitheater's steps and then descended the dune on the other side. Thistle held Dora's hand tight as they walked up the beach to where the carriage waited, light spilling out from its open front. The air smelled of spices and frying fish.

The troupe turned their heads as Dora and Thistle walked toward them. Neither Director nor Nestor spoke, but they sat up very straight in their seats.

Thistle stopped next to the fire. Without speaking, he rolled up his left sleeve. The thick leaves and stems shone against his arm. The thistles weren't pretty; they were jagged and warped. Thistle rolled up his other sleeve, then held out his arms, hands clenched into fists.

"Here they are," he said.

"May I touch them?" Nestor asked.

Nestor held out one hand, palm down. Thistle took it and hesitantly placed it on his forearm. His own hands were trembling.

Nestor closed his eyes. Then he nodded and removed his hand.

"It will work," he said. "Her essence is all over these."

Thistle quickly rolled his sleeves back down and stuck his hands into his armpits.

Nestor smiled at Thistle. "Thank you, lad. I know that was very difficult."

Thistle nodded curtly.

"Because she left her mark, she is inextricably linked to you," Nestor said. "We can trace your scars back to her. However . . ." He paused.

"However?" Thistle said.

"All places have time, just not always the same time," Nestor said. "I cannot tell you exactly when you will find her. We are operating at a different scale out here. A long time may have passed since Augusta left the Gardens."

"It doesn't matter. So long as I find her," Thistle said.

Nestor looked up at Director, who nodded.

"Colleagues!" Director announced. "We shall perform a montage."

The troupe packed everything into the carriage and closed the wall. Inside, they arranged the sofa and armchairs in a circle. Apprentice rolled out the flat map in the center; Director and Nestor came carrying the canopy and set it on top. They spent a long moment fiddling with the canopy's legs.

"Ready?" Director said.

"Ready," Nestor replied.

They let go of the canopy and stood up. It hummed to life. Inside, the multitude of spheres and discs that hung from strings in the canopy's ceiling lit up. Little clouds and swirls moved between them.

"Please, have a seat." Director sat down in the nearest armchair.

Dora and Thistle sat on the sofa. An excited-looking Apprentice plonked herself down next to Dora. She was holding a small lyre.

Nestor stepped into the circle. He was dressed in heavy robes that left his right shoulder and arm bare, and wore a crown set with rows of horns. His beard and hair had grown into long corkscrew curls. His eyes, when he turned his head to the audience, were fixed on a point far away.

"I am the creator, the omniscient, the lord of stories. I will tell you of how Augusta Prima of the Gardens was found."

Apprentice plucked a quiet rain of notes from the lyre.

Nestor closed his eyes. "The Troupe traveled through creation, searching for the villain that had caused such grievous harm to their young friends. At first they knew not where Augusta had gone, for the worlds are many. But then young Thistle showed where Augusta had marked his flesh and created a connection to herself. And so the Troupe set sail, letting young Thistle's scars lead them to their goal. And here they are, soaring through the cosmos."

A shining blob, a wheel of sorts, blinked into existence in the map. It floated through the arrangement of spheres and discs, up and down, in loops and spirals. Looking at it made Dora feel queasy. She glanced at Thistle, who was rubbing his left forearm, and put her hand over his to stop him. He leaned his head against her shoulder but didn't relax.

"They skirted formless shoals, planet nurseries, wastelands, and primordial pools. They saw a city of brass, a city of rain, a city of clay. Finally, artwork called to maker: this was where the Troupe made port."

The little wheel stopped at a small swirled sphere close to the bottom of the map and hovered there. Nestor bowed and backed out of the circle. Apprentice put down her harp.

"Here we are," Director said.

She pointed at the sphere. "That there is Earth. And those"— she pointed to a protrusion on the surface of the sphere—"are the Gardens. Like a boil."

The protrusion looked like it was pulsing.

"Anyway, that's not where we are going," Director said. "We have arrived at our destination."

Apprentice and Journeyman folded the carriage wall aside.

19

Nils's plate was full with pölsa and potatoes.

"I don't trust you to eat well," Johanna of Avastugan's farm said.

Nils chuckled. "I don't eat as well as you," he said, and put the first forkful in his mouth.

Johanna's pölsa was famous. The balance of innards, meat, barley grain, and onions was perfect, and the potatoes she served with it were small and tender. She had even put a slice of fried pork on the side. Nils thought to himself that he could eat her pölsa every day of the week.

Johanna sat down across the table. Her kitchen was nothing like Nils's kitchen; the floor had been scrubbed until it shone and the curtains in the window were washed and ironed. She was very well-kept herself, short but strong, with deep laugh lines and quick, efficient movements. Every once in a while, Nils came down to her farm for supper or fika. Slightly more often now that her husband had passed. Johanna had confessed, no, openly stated that she felt lonely too now that her daughters had also left. *We need company, you and I,* she had said.

"How are your boys?" she asked.

"Nothing new," Nils said. "Olof and Erik are both doing well. They send letters now and then. They haven't had leave all summer, and they're bored, but that's all right. Bored is better."

Johanna nodded. "Better than the alternative. I'm glad I had only girls."

They ate in silence for a while. Then Johanna said, "Do you think the war will come here?"

"Who knows?" Nils said. "Norway is occupied. We're only a day's walk from the border. All the Germans have to do is move east."

"My sister sent me a letter," Johanna said. "She said her youngest doesn't have any shoes. And that they barely have enough to eat. I might smuggle some things across the border. I did it this spring. I can do it again."

"You would be putting yourself in danger," Nils said.

"Eh," Johanna replied. "Who's going to suspect an old woman?"

Johanna was thrifty and resourceful. She sent cream and meat to her daughters in Stockholm by mail, even though it was prohibited. She labeled the packages BOOKS. Apparently one of the packages had started bleeding once, but the ladies at the post office in Stockholm had laughed about "gory crime novels" and let it through. Everyone helped one another out in these times.

"There," Johanna said, and pushed her plate away. She put a piece of her precious tobacco under her lip. "That's better."

Nils mopped the remaining pölsa from his plate with a piece of bread. "Thank you, Johanna. Delicious as always."

"Did you know Berit found a downed parachute the other day?" Johanna said. "Pure silk. Us neighbors divided it between us. Everyone's wearing fancy blouses for church now. Why don't you come to church sometime?"

"You know I'm not much of a churchgoer," Nils mumbled.

"It's not just about God," Johanna said. "Who has time for God? I have work to do. But you get to meet people."

Nils shrugged. "I'm not much of a people person either."

"You get to meet me," Johanna said, and smiled.

Sometimes Nils thought about asking Johanna for more than just friendship. She was a good woman. But he didn't know how to ask. Perhaps she was asking him, now. It made him flustered.

"I have to go," he said, and stood up. "I have to make it home in time for milking."

Johanna looked a little disappointed but nodded. "Cows won't wait."

She waved him off as he climbed onto his bicycle and started his journey back home. It was a long way to go, and it was uphill, but he was full of pölsa and good company.

Johanna was right; Nils was lonely. It was difficult to work up the will to do the cooking and housework for just one person. There were no lodgers this year—the tourists had stopped coming. Nils had only been down to the village below a few times to get mail and buy necessities. Sometimes the couple that called themselves Grandmother and Grandfather came to visit, strange folk from the other side of the mountain. Nils had never quite figured out what they were. It would have been impolite to ask. He hadn't seen them for months now.

He might be going a little stir-crazy. A couple of weeks ago he had caught a fever, fainted, and woken up on the kitchen floor. What if he had become really ill? No one would have found him for weeks. After that fall, there were the dreams. He dreamed that he was a woman; he dreamed of a timeless garden, of riches and luxury he had never seen; he dreamed that he danced in the twilight. And then he dreamed about walking through a city, and catching a train, and walking out onto the bog, where he met a man who looked very much like himself. Then he would wake up, unsure of who he was.

And sometimes he found himself standing between the privy and the house, or on his way to the barn, not knowing how long he had been there, humming a strange tune to a beat he had never heard before: *one-two-three-four-five, one-two-three-four-five-six, one-two-three* . . . and there was a dance that came along with it, but his feet were too heavy, his legs too stiff. His mouth warped the tune into something plain. Then the song would be gone again, elusive like smoke. As if he had been someone else, once. Someone powerful.

Elna, had she still been alive, would have frowned at him and told him to stop being ridiculous. She was good like that. Had been good to him for twenty-four years, since he first came to the village and caught her eye. There had been a harvest feast. They had danced all night, and Elna had joked that he must be one of the fair folk to dance so well. But he had said no, he was Nils Nilsson, and that was all. She had smiled at him and said that was good enough for her. Olof and Erik, when they arrived, had her eyes.

Now Nils was on his own until his sons came home or the Germans knocked on the door. In the meantime, he would go about his chores. And perhaps go see Johanna a little more often.

20

The house-carriage sat on a blunt hilltop, its stairs unfolded. Mountains lay low and wide against the horizon. Between the mountains, Dora could see flat woodland and bogs, and hundreds of little lakes. Patches of snow dotted the slopes. The world looked hazy, as if it were raining, but no drops fell on the carriage's roof. Somehow, Dora knew what those bogs would feel like under her feet; she knew their scents and their sounds, and the animals they hid. She knew that the stream running into the valley below would taste like ice and stone.

"Does this look right?" Director said.

"It looks like home," Dora said.

Thistle shaded his eyes with his hand. "How do we know Augusta is here?"

Director shrugged. "According to you, she is. Somewhere close, at least." She pointed. "There's a farm down there. It's a start."

Thistle stared at the landscape, clenching his fists.

"What will you do once you find her?" Journeyman asked.

"Ask her for my name back," Thistle said.

"That's it?"

Thistle nodded.

"And you think she'll just answer?"

"It's the only chance I have."

"Fair enough." Journeyman looked doubtful.

Dora stepped out of the carriage, down the stairs, and onto the rock.

"Stop!" Apprentice shouted. "We're not there yet! We're only backstage. All the people are frontstage."

Dora quickly climbed back up.

"What?" Thistle said.

"We move through the backdrop of the universe," Director said. "We need to lift the veil so that you can go through."

Nestor joined them on the stairs. He had shrunk, as had his beard, and he was once again the kindly old gentleman.

"Here we are," Nestor said. "At the right place, hopefully at the right time. Keep in mind what I said."

Thistle nodded. "I just want to find her," he said.

"Very well," Director said. "Let us send the children on their way."

"Can I go?" Apprentice said. "Just to have a look."

"You have work to do," Director replied.

Apprentice made a whining noise. "Please. I won't be a minute. Just a peek."

"No," Director said firmly.

Apprentice looked at Nestor, who shook his head. "Don't look at me. Director said no."

Apprentice pouted and kicked the couch.

There was a rustle from inside the carriage. Journeyman came out with an armful of pipes and flutes.

"Are these appropriate?" he asked.

"Very," Director said. "I'll take the aulos."

"Crumhorn, please," Nestor said.

Journeyman shared out the instruments to the others: a strange double flute for the Director, a long curved wooden flute for Nestor, and a tin whistle for Apprentice. He kept a long birch-bark trumpet for himself.

"What do we do if we need to find you again?" Thistle said.

"Go to the crossroads and ask for us," Director said. "Very simple."

Journeyman walked over to where Dora was standing. He tentatively held out his arms. Dora stepped into his embrace and rested her chin on his shoulder. She ran her hand down his back and felt the hum of myriad possible shapes waiting under his skin. He smelled like he had by the pool in the woods: urgent, musky.

Journeyman drew a shaky breath and held her closer. "I wish you would stay."

Dora closed her eyes and ran a hand through his hair, cradled the back of his head.

"I know," she said. "Thank you."

"It's time to go." Thistle's voice, his touch on her arm.

Dora extricated herself from Journeyman's embrace. His face was wet. He held on to one of her hands.

"Don't forget me," he said.

She shook her head.

"It had to happen sometime," Director mumbled behind her.

"At least it was someone kind," Nestor mumbled back.

"Now, stand back," Director said in a louder voice, and waved Dora and Thistle toward the edge of the stage.

"How does this work?" Thistle asked.

"It's a musical number," Nestor said cheerfully. "The music that moves the world."

"One, two, three," Director said, and raised the double flute to her mouth.

The collected sound from the four instruments was deafening, a warped tune that bounced around the walls of the theater. The noise invaded Dora's body, its vibrations beating against her chest. Thistle grabbed her arm, and she looked down at him. He pointed at the landscape.

The haze that had obscured the mountainside was lifting; beyond, a yellow sun turned snow patches and lakes into shards of light that left spots on Dora's vision. Dora looked back at the troupe. Director nodded. Dora took Thistle's hand and descended the stairs. She caught Thistle as he jumped down onto the rocks. The noise from the company was still too loud for them to speak. They walked down the hill, into the sun, and the music ended abruptly.

A hand that wasn't Thistle's patted Dora on the shoulder, and she turned around. It was Apprentice, flute in hand, an exhilarated smile on her face. Behind them, the carriage had disappeared from view; there was just the mountain.

"Ha!" Apprentice shouted. "I did it!"

"What?" Dora said.

"I wanted to have a look," Apprentice said. "I'm having a look!"

"I thought you weren't supposed to," Thistle said.

"Oh, don't be like that," Apprentice said. "I'm just sightseeing."

She put the tin whistle to her lips and played a little victorious tune.

The air trembled, and then the ground.

Apprentice's eyes widened. "Maybe I shouldn't have played it on this side."

The mountain moved under their feet.

21

Nils was in the barn, resting his forehead against Svana's warm flank as he milked her, when he heard the sound of thunder. He went outside and looked up at the clear sky. Then he saw it: a massive cloud of dust rising up from the side of Koryggen Mountain. A rockslide. He should go and have a look when he was done.

He went back into the barn and milked Rosa as well, then emptied the bucket into the milk can and went outside to put the can to cool in the stream. The cows were happy to leave the barn and go graze in the paddock.

Nils ate his breakfast as quickly as he could, then took his bicycle out of the shed. He rode west up the mountain and through the pass between it and the hill next to it, where the road ended at an old abandoned barn. He leaned his bicycle against the wall and walked up the slope. It wasn't long before he spotted the rockslide.

Some of the boulders were as big as his privy, but mostly there was smaller rubble. Among the rocks, a blue shape. It did look like someone. Nils made his way over the rocks, careful lest he disturb them again.

At first, Nils thought it was in fact two people, the smaller one curled up against the bigger. When he looked again, it was just an unconscious boy in blue coveralls next to a vaguely human-shaped boulder. His right leg was soaked with blood, and his face was covered in cuts. His eyes fluttered open, and he whispered something in a hoarse voice. A little ways off, Nils saw a hand sticking out of the rubble. Nils rolled one of the rocks aside. A smashed face framed by tangled hair stared blindly into nothing.

"Help," the boy mumbled.

Nils left the other body and moved closer to the boy.

"Don't worry," Nils told him. "We'll sort you out. I'm Nils. What's your name?"

The boy looked up at him but said nothing.

The boy stiffened as Nils got his hunting knife out of his belt, but relaxed a little when Nils merely cut his pant leg open. The wound was deep, right across the shin, but the bone didn't seem to be broken.

"How did you end up here?" Nils asked.

The boy didn't respond.

Nils carefully took off the boy's boot and felt his foot. It was warm and pink. He nodded to himself.

"Good," he said. "Your leg will be all right."

"Please don't hurt me," the boy said.

"Of course not," Nils replied. "Now let's see if we can get you up."

"My sister," the boy whispered.

"Where's your sister?" Nils said.

"She was here . . ." The boy trailed off.

The other body.

The boy didn't need to know about that right now.

"Don't you worry about your sister," Nils said.

Nils took his scarf and put a makeshift bandage around the boy's leg. Nils put the boot back on, then helped the boy sit up.

"Let's get you indoors," Nils said.

The boy was heavier than he looked, but Nils managed to get him onto the rack of his bicycle. He wrapped the boy's arms around his own waist, told him to hold on tight, and trudged homeward.

Elna had never let anything go to waste. Half the chest of drawers in the attic was filled with scraps of old bedsheets and clothes too worn to mend. Elna would turn sheets into pillowcases and the pillowcases into handkerchiefs and, when that didn't work, wraps. She had kept the bandages that she'd wrapped around their sons' navel stumps when they were born. Even after she died, Nils couldn't bring himself to throw them away. They were so soft that Nils could barely feel them in his hand. He plucked what cobwebs he could find from the windowsills and corners—cobwebs prevented wounds going bad, he knew that much—and went back downstairs.

The boy wept as Nils cleaned his leg, but he made no noise, just gripped the bed frame until it creaked. When the wound was clean, Nils squeezed the edges together and covered them in cobweb, then wrapped the leg with the old bandages.

"There," he said. "All done. Now let's hope there won't be an infection."

He cleaned up the boy's face. The cuts were many but shallow, and looked like they would heal on their own.

"I'll need to feel your belly," Nils said. "Make sure nothing's broken in there."

As he tried to unbutton the boy's clothes, the boy resisted.

"Very well," Nils said. "I understand modesty. Let me at least feel it."

The boy lay back, eyes still fixed on the wall. Nils lightly prodded his abdomen and then his ribs. The boy wasn't coughing blood and his belly wasn't hard.

Nils nodded to himself. "You will be all right. We just need to make sure to keep that leg clean."

He unfolded a blanket and draped it over the boy, then added a sheepskin.

"Where is my sister?" the boy asked.

Nils couldn't bring himself to say it. "She's outside," he said instead, which was true.

"I need her."

"I'll tell her you asked for her."

"Good," the boy said, and promptly fell asleep.

The boy slept all day. Nils went about his daily tasks, mulling the whole thing over. He should really go down to the village right away, ask about the boy he had found. But he couldn't just leave the boy alone. It could wait until tomorrow. And the girl wasn't going anywhere.

In the evening, Nils bedded down on the kitchen bench and listened to the boy's breath. Outside, the meadows and moors lay quiet save for the occasional small animal noise. This was the best time of year, the best time of day, when everything was alive but asleep; the sun just below the horizon, and the sky alight. It was the perfect light for dancing, had he been young. Nils hummed his song, *one-two-three-four-five, one-two-three-four-five-six*, tapping his knuckle on the wooden armrest, but he couldn't fathom where he'd learned the tune.

22

The boy was sitting up in bed when Nils entered the chamber the next morning. There was nothing left but to tell the truth.

"I'm sorry, lad," Nils said. "Your sister is dead."

The boy stared at him. "You said she was on the mountain."

"She was. I saw her," Nils replied. "She didn't survive."

The boy's eyes emptied of all life, and his face went slack.

"I couldn't tell you yesterday," Nils continued. "You were too weak."

"Where is she?" the boy whispered.

Nils hesitated, then said: "She's buried on the mountain." It wasn't a lie, after all.

"I want to see," the boy said. "I need to see."

"It's too far," Nils said. "Your leg needs to heal. Soon."

The boy didn't scream or cry; he sagged back against the pillow and stared into empty space.

·

He didn't speak for a few days after that. He didn't drink or eat on his own, but opened his mouth for the spoonfuls of gruel that Nils fed him. Nils sat by the bed and read to him from the books his sons had once enjoyed: *Gulliver's Travels*, *Robinson Crusoe*, *The Wonderful Adventures of Nils*. If the boy listened, he didn't show it, but Nils persisted.

Nils was true to his word. When the wound on the boy's leg had closed, he brought him outside for the first time. They walked to a pile of rocks on the nearest hill, Nils supporting the boy on his arm. It was a tourist spot, really; hikers would place a rock at the top as a sign that they had been there. They had done so for decades, and the pile was high enough to look like a little cairn.

"This is where you can mourn your sister," he told the boy.

The boy sat down by the rocks, face just as empty as it had been for the last week. He was motionless until the sun started to dip toward the horizon and a cold wind blew in.

After that, the boy showed no sign of wanting to leave; he showed no sign of wanting anything. He sat in the kitchen or on the bench outside the house. Nils knew that he should have reported the event to the authorities, but something stopped him. If he did, they would take the boy away. And Nils very much wanted to keep the boy. There was just something about him.

August segued into September. Nils didn't mind the boy's apathy. He fed him, made sure he was warm, made sure he bathed every now and then. The boy refused to let Nils see him without clothes, though, always keeping his sleeves rolled down and his shirt well tucked into the trousers Nils had given him. Nils let the boy wash himself in the bedchamber with the door closed. The boy wouldn't shave, would in fact shy away from anything that looked like a knife, and grew a scraggly auburn beard.

He seemed to like the cows. He started following Nils into the barn in the mornings; at first, he merely stood by the wall and watched as Nils milked the cows. Then one day he put a hand on Rosa's neck, and she let him. After that, whenever Nils had been in town or to see Johanna, he would come home to find the boy in the barn, quietly running a brush over a cow's flank.

The boy wouldn't talk about his past, or give his name, and Nils didn't press the issue. He would talk when he wanted to. These things could take time. From the looks of it, he had been to hell and back.

In October the boy was still there, a quiet presence. Nils had put off checking on his sister's body for so long that it by now seemed pointless. She would be devoured by birds and foxes. It was the way of things. Neither had he told Johanna or anyone else about the boy. He found that it wasn't hard to keep that particular secret.

The day came when the boy sat down on a milking stool of his own accord. After that, he took over the morning milking. Nils showed him how to make cheese and filbunke from the milk. It turned out that the boy was a fast learner. He went from sitting by the stove for hours every day to spending just the evenings there. He still wouldn't smile, but there was a different air about him, as if he had started to breathe properly.

÷

But there were changes that came with the boy's recuperation. Nils found a cache in the bedroom where the boy had squirreled away some things: a spare shirt, socks, a box of matches. As if he was planning to go somewhere. When confronted with this, the boy merely shrugged and said that they might come in handy. Nils put them back in their original places. But after that, when going into the room, he would find things: a rope under the mattress, clean socks in a corner. The boy merely watched as he took the things away. Nils had to do this again and again. It was like this with boys. You had to be consistent.

Temperatures had dropped dramatically in the past week, and the first snow lay in thick drifts around the house. Nils and the boy had potatoes and the last of the salted pork for supper, washed down with barley coffee. Nils pushed his plate away.

"I'm going into the village tomorrow," he said. "We need to stock up for winter."

"Take me with you," the boy said.

Nils glanced at him. "Why?" he asked.

"I just thought it was time," the boy replied. "I think my sister would have wanted me to go on."

"Go on to do what?" Nils asked.

"There's someone I need to find."

"Who?"

The boy wouldn't meet his eyes. "Someone," he said.

"And do you think that this someone is in the village?"

"No, but it's a start."

"There's nothing there to see," Nils said. "Just some houses and a general store."

"I think it's time for me to go see it. I have things to do."

"You're better off staying here," Nils said.

"But I want to—"

"I said no!"

The boy shrunk back, and Nils realized he had been shouting.

"I have to try," the boy said, very quietly. "It's time."

"We'll talk about it in the morning."

The boy went out to milk the cows. Nils washed the dishes. Why had he been shouting? Why was it so important to keep the boy here? It just was. But this anger didn't feel like him. Nils had never raised his voice to anyone in his life. He tried to shrug it off, sharpened a pencil, and wrote a shopping list. He'd have to borrow Andersson's horse and cart if he wanted to get everything home in one go. Maybe see Johanna on the way into town. She would be happy to make him lunch. He should talk to Persson about borrowing his bull while he was in town, too. It was time to have at least Svana covered.

Nils couldn't really afford to feed another mouth. Except maybe if the owner of that mouth earned his keep. The boy could certainly earn his keep, if only he'd stay.

If only he'd stay. But he'd want to leave as soon as he saw the village.

After all Nils had done for him, the boy had no right to leave. He belonged to this house now. There was that thought again. Why was it important to keep the boy? He just had to. Nils folded up the list, put it in his breast pocket, and picked up a worn sock from the mending basket.

The boy came back inside, bringing the smell of night air and cow dung. He drank the barley coffee Nils had made, sat in silence on the kitchen bench for a while and watched Nils darn the sock, then went to bed.

It wasn't long before the breaths in the bedchamber lengthened. Nils got up from the kitchen bench and quietly locked the door. Then he went outside, closed the chamber's window shutters, and barred them with a plank.

The air was cold and clear. Faint waves of green light swept across the sky. It reminded him of something. It made him want to dance. Perhaps the boy would be in a better mood if they had a little party. A real party, with sweets and wine and dancing.

Back in the kitchen, he made himself a fresh cup of barley coffee. He made a new list of things to buy in the village. Sweets and wine. Let them wonder. He didn't care. Should he see Johanna? Perhaps not. It was too important to get food for the feast.

They were going to have a feast, the boy and he.

23

The smell of rock. Hard things digging into her back. Dora opened her eyes and saw nothing.

She lay on her side, embedded in something heavy. She could breathe but it was hard to move. Heart pounding, she flexed her arms and legs; they creaked and popped, as if she had lain still for a long time. Dora reached upward with a grunt, digging through the cold mass until her hand suddenly felt nothing. She gathered her legs under her and pushed herself upright.

Dora was standing on a mountainside, in a hollow that had filled with snow. The mountainside above looked like it had collapsed, and she herself was at the edge of the rocks that had spilled out from its wound. The shape of the rockslide was softened by the blanket of snow that covered everything. Below, warped and angry-looking trees dotted the slope.

"Thistle?" Dora called. "Apprentice?"

There was no reply. A few steps away, something like a twig

stuck out of the snow. Dora climbed over the rubble toward it. Her limbs were so stiff it hurt. How long had she lain there?

The twig was a near-skeletal arm, wrapped in tatters of blue cloth. Its fingers were missing. Dora flung the rubble aside. Half-covered by a large stone lay a corpse dressed in blue coveralls. Long strands of dark blond hair clung to its skull. Those were Apprentice's coveralls. That was her ruined face, eyes eaten away, lips receded from her teeth.

"Apprentice?" Dora said.

Apprentice's corpse stared back at her with empty sockets. She had been so happy about going on an adventure. No more adventures for her now.

"I'm sorry," she said to Apprentice. "I hope it was quick." Then she called out, "Thistle?"

The rounded hilltops looked soft, as if smoothed down by giants. A carpet of fir trees covered the valley's bottom. The cloud cover was thin and low.

"Thistle!" she called again. "Thistle! Thistle!"

A fat white bird on the ground stared at her and wandered off.

Dora walked around the rockslide in a spiral, lifting rocks, searching for traces of Thistle. There were none. No tracks in the snow except for hers. She returned to where Apprentice lay and picked her up. Only the blue coveralls held the body together.

"I'm sorry," she said to Apprentice. "It won't be a proper funeral."

Dora walked to a flat area, put Apprentice down, and dug into the snow with her fingers until she felt hardened dirt. Even frozen, this earth felt familiar. The smell, the feel. It told her that even though it would soften for her, the soil here was too meager for a burial.

Not too meager for her birth. Dora had first come to consciousness in a place like this.

÷

"Wake up," a voice had said. "Wake up, child."

And Dora had woken up, climbed out of the soil that smelled and felt just like here. Long hands had caught her. The morning sun had warmed her skin. The tall woman had looked down at her with burning eyes.

"Look at you," Ghorbi had said. "You're perfect. Let's get you to your father."

Dora shook off the memory and picked up Apprentice again, trudging through the snow away from the rockslide. She would find better ground for Apprentice while searching for Thistle. She would go into the valley. Thistle would have done the same.

Wading through the snow was slow going, but the work made the stiffness go away. Dora's breath left her mouth in thick clouds. Frost gathered on her eyelashes. Apprentice's hair swayed in the wind. There were no sounds except those that Dora made, and even those were muted by the snow. She made her way past twisted birch trees that glittered with ice; then the pine forest took over as she came to the bottom of the valley. The snow cover was thinner here, which made it easier to walk. A tree had fallen over, its roots pointing into the sky. Dora dug into the hollow underneath, into the cold ground, and lay Apprentice down. She adjusted Apprentice's body so that she almost looked asleep. A flat rock under her head and her hair untangled, and it was done. Dora lifted her hands, and the frozen soil enveloped Apprentice's body. Apprentice would be part of this land now.

The slope steepened slightly as Dora walked farther in among the trees, into a sharp scent of needles and sap. At the very bottom of the valley, a stream flowed down a rocky riverbed, too swift to freeze in the middle. Dora crouched by a little pool, punched a hole through the ice, and stuck her hands in the water. It tasted like she knew it would, of winter and minerals. If Thistle had come this way, he would have stopped to drink, and he would have complained about the cold water. There was a little wooden bridge. Dora crossed it.

The light gradually waned, but Dora had no trouble finding her way between the trees; her feet and nose and ears told her what her eyes didn't, as if she was made for finding her way here. She trudged up the other slope, among firs that stood so close together that Dora saw the opening in the mountainside only when the tree line abruptly ended.

Boulders were piled up and scattered around the hole in the rock. The snow on the ground here was patterned with footprints, human and something else. A light glowed inside. And Dora could hear, faintly, the flat clank of bells.

As Dora came closer to the opening, she could sense that it was the flickering sheen of an open fire, accompanied by a rich smell of baking bread that made her stomach twist. The voices of a man and a woman. They were laughing. It wasn't the demented cackle of lords and ladies, nor the troupe's eerie giggle. These people laughed like Dora and Thistle did with each other.

As Dora reached the opening, it was as if she could almost see them. The tunnel sloped downward into a cavern with rushes on the floor. There was the heavy sound of a hoof scraping on the ground, deep animal calls, a bell. Dora slipped on a rock. It skipped down the tunnel with a loud noise.

The light went out. The voices and bells disappeared. The tunnel gaped at her.

"I'm looking for my brother," Dora called into the emptiness. "That's all I want."

Silence.

"He's hurt," Dora continued. "He needs me."

Nothing happened. Dora sat down on a boulder with her back to the cave. Her eyes prickled.

"You seem lost," someone said behind her.

Dora turned her head. The light from the cave had returned, and revealed a broad-shouldered woman. Her skirt and the long shawl tied across her chest were red. Under the embroidered headscarf, her face was strong-jawed and stern. Then she smiled, and her features folded into laugh lines.

She bent down. "Don't cry, girl. Now, tell me what you call yourself."

"Dora."

"Well met, Dora. You may call me Grandmother."

"That's not a name," Dora said.

Grandmother smiled again. "You're right, it's not. We don't hand our names out just like that."

"Why did you disappear?"

"We had to have a look at you first," the woman replied. "Of course, then you told us why you were here. We've decided you're a good sort."

Grandmother held out her hand. Dora took it, and Grandmother helped her upright without effort. Then she turned and walked down the tunnel at a brisk pace. Something like a tail peeked out from under her skirt. At the bottom of the slope, the tunnel widened into a chamber lit by lanterns hanging from the ceiling. Four fat white animals lay or stood on the straw-covered floor, chewing cud. One of them wore a large silver bell that clanked as it stuck her head into the long feeding trough that ran the length of the chamber. The air was warm and close and smelled of dung, but it was a safe smell.

"Move over, Stjärna."

Grandmother slapped the hindquarters of the beast standing in the middle of the space. Stjärna took a step to the side and went over to sniff Dora with her wet muzzle.

"Don't mind the cow; she's just curious," Grandmother said over her shoulder.

Dora patted Stjärna's neck. She seemed content with this and walked over to the feeding trough.

"Do you always keep them in here?" Dora asked.

"Only at night and in winter," Grandmother replied. She moved across the chamber to an opening on the other side, waving for Dora to follow. "This used to be a mine. The miners moved out, so we moved in."

The next tunnel bent to the right and opened into another chamber that was a little larger than the first. There was a roaring fireplace, next to which stood a four-poster bed. Around the large table in the middle of the room were chairs and a wood-framed sofa. By the fireplace stood a man in moleskin trousers and a long waistcoat the same color as Grandmother's shawl. He turned around as Dora and Grandmother came in.

"Dora, this is Grandfather," said Grandmother, and took off her scarf.

Grandfather gave Dora a slight bow, then walked closer. He was as weathered as Grandmother, with gray hair that curled around his ears.

"Good evening, Dora," he said.

The lines around Grandfather's eyes were not from laughing, and they didn't soften much when he smiled.

"She's looking for her brother," Grandmother said.

Grandfather nodded. "And where did you lose him?"

"We fell down the mountain, and when I woke up he wasn't there. Is he here? He needs me," Dora said.

Grandfather and Grandmother exchanged glances.

Then Grandmother said, "We saw a girl-shaped stone on the mountain. There was a girl corpse there, too. We didn't touch it. You don't look like a ghost, so you must be the stone girl."

"There was no one there who could have been your brother," Grandfather said.

"I have to go to him," Dora said.

"Dora," Grandfather said. "It has been a while. That was in harvest season. It is winter now, although it came too early."

"What?" Dora said, and her head buzzed. "So he could be dead. On the mountain."

"Or not," Grandmother replied. "A man lives not far from there. He might have taken the boy in. I don't know; we haven't seen him for some time. We'll visit him tomorrow."

"You should sit down, Dora," Grandfather said. "You must be starving. There's no use worrying about your brother now."

Dora's head was still buzzing, but her stomach rumbled in reply. Grandfather smiled.

They sat her down in one of the chairs by the table and draped a thick shawl over her shoulders, even though Dora protested she didn't feel cold. Grandfather put a large wooden bowl of porridge in the center of the table and handed Grandmother and Dora a spoon each, then made a little pit in the middle of the bowl. Grandmother lifted the lid on a box sitting on the table and dug out a large lump of butter, which she dropped into the pit.

"Go on," Grandmother said, and gestured at the bowl, where the butter was melting into a little puddle.

Dora glanced at the little tip of tail that peeked out from beneath Grandmother's skirt, and for a moment forgot about Thistle.

"What are you?"

Grandfather laughed, an unexpected sound. "We're vittra, my dear. The hidden folk. What about you?"

"I don't know what I am," Dora replied.

"She does have an odd accent," Grandmother remarked. "Are you from very far away, then?"

"I don't know how far it is," Dora said.

She brought the spoon to her mouth. The porridge tasted of oats and honey and salty butter, and it settled comfortably in her stomach.

"Who is the man you talked about?" Dora said after she had swallowed.

"Nils Nilsson," Grandfather said. "Honest fellow."

"A little odd," Grandmother filled in. "Fairy blood, I always thought. His wife was a good woman, too. She borrowed Stjärna when their sons were little. Never have I seen someone take such good care of a cow."

Dora put the spoon down. "Please take me there. Now. I need to know if he is alive."

Grandmother put her hand on Dora's. "No rush, dear. We'll take you there in the morning. We can't cross the mountain at night. If your brother was lost on the mountain, he is already dead. But if someone found him, he's all right, and it can wait until tomorrow."

Grandmother and Grandfather let Dora have the butter in the middle. They asked her where she came from, and Dora told them of the Gardens and their masters, and how she was grown from a seed, or at least that's what Ghorbi had told her. And she told them about Thistle, her brother, a stolen child. Grandmother and Grandfather listened in silence, with raised eyebrows.

"Well," Grandfather said. "That's a strange story."

Grandmother nodded. "Indeed."

Dora yawned. She was still anxious, but so tired.

"You need to sleep, properly this time. Turning to stone is no way to sleep," Grandmother said.

They unfolded the kitchen bench for her and bedded her down among blankets that smelled of sheep. Dora drifted off to the low sound of Grandmother and Grandfather talking.

24

Nils set off when it was still dark. He made the hour-long walk over to Andersson's, where he borrowed the horse and cart. Then he went into the village and bought what he needed. Goods for the coming winter, and some fancy things. Let people talk.

By the time Nils finally returned, unloaded the cart, and put the horse in the stable, the boy had almost managed to knock the door off its hinges. But the house was sturdy.

"Why are you doing this?" the boy sobbed from inside.

"I can't have you leave," Nils replied. "I bought sweets. We're going to have a party."

A party needed decoration, and this place was a dull one. Nils went through chests and cupboards, and eventually found old tablecloths and dresses. They made for fine curtains and drapes. He nailed them to doors and walls, adjusting them until he was satisfied. There were no flowers to find this time of year, but he went out and cut some birch branches that he nailed to the ceiling and adorned with some of the Christmas decorations from the attic. It began to feel festive. He found his best suit. It was not very well cut, and the fabric was dull. But he found some leftover paint from the barn with which he drew gaudy swirls of flowers over the back of the jacket. Then he put it on. There was something in the jacket's breast pocket, and he drew it out. A golden locket: a watch. Elna had given him this for their wedding. He hadn't seen it for a long time. The engraved flowers on the lid tickled his fingers. He briefly held it against his cheek, feeling the metal warm to his skin, then put it back. A wash and a shave, and he was ready for the party.

The boy made no attempt to fight as Nils unlocked the door and entered the bedchamber, just sat in a corner of the room, staring.

"Are you hungry?" Nils asked.

"Who are you?" the boy said quietly. "Who are you really?"

Nils tilted his head. "Whatever do you mean? I am as you see me."

"Yes, you are as I see you. I see someone else than the man who took me in." The boy's stare was forward, too forward, the stare of someone who needed to be chastised.

Nils blinked. *Someone else than the man who took me in.* Perhaps he was. Yes, he was. Something had been growing inside him, something strange yet familiar. Something old. It was right. He knew what to say; the words rolled off his tongue.

"You'll want to be nice, my sweet," Nils replied. "I want a nice party. Just you and me. We'll dance!"

He took a couple of dance steps, clapped a rhythm with his

hands: one-two-three-four-five, one-two-three-four-five-six. The boy put a hand over his mouth.

"You—" he said through his fingers.

Yes. Nils slapped the boy with the back of his hand. The boy let out a muted cry and crawled farther into the corner.

"That's no way to address me, lad," Nils said. "What do we say?"

"My lord?" the boy whispered. "I beg your pardon, my lord. I did not mean to offend. Please forgive me."

The boy bowed his head and held his hands out, palms up, in a gesture that was so, so familiar. And there, on his wrist, a scar peeked out. Nils knew what that was. It would be a stem, a flower stem, curling up around the boy's arm and on across his shoulder and chest. Such a beautiful flower.

Nils tilted his head. "I know you," he said.

He bent down, tore the boy's shirt open, and recognized his own handiwork. And, finally, the boy.

"Thistle," he said. "I know you. You're all grown up."

"Augusta," Thistle breathed, then screamed.

Nils went to the hallway mirror and studied his own face. Deep lines crisscrossed his skin, and his eyes were watery. His mouth was full of teeth with receding gums. His hair looked dull and was going gray. Everything was too worn, too big, too base.

He was not supposed to look like this. She was not supposed to look like this. She, Augusta of the Gardens. This body was strong, yes, but awkward and heavy and old. Joints and tendons ached and complained. A couple of teeth felt loose. It was a body that wouldn't last. Augusta remembered herself now, and Phantasos. He had come here to live out his life as a mortal man. He had found Elna, married her, raised two boys. He had abandoned who he once was. And then Augusta had come along. She had killed him, and he had cursed her to live out his life. And maybe she would have, had not Thistle found her. He had recognized her, but it had not turned her back into her old self. One of your own, Phantasos had said. It had to be one of her own. How had Thistle found her?

The cows were lowing in the barn. They wanted milking, of course. Menial work, not fit for a lady of Augusta's standing. She ignored the noise and went inside the kitchen. Thistle didn't talk back when she told him to put the feast in order.

On the kitchen table, Thistle laid out the things Augusta had bought in the village: soft bread and honey; little cakes, ham, tiny sausages; a bottle of spirits. He was a good boy. She allowed him to sit at the table, even have a taste of the bread. He sat slumped on his stool, legs squeezed together, hugging himself.

"How did you get here?" Augusta said conversationally.

"I ran away, my lady," Thistle mumbled.

Augusta paused. "You ran away?"

Thistle nodded.

"If you found your way out, you can find your way back in. How? Tell me how." Augusta leaned closer and grabbed him by his collar. "Mnemosyne cast me out. She had no right. You will answer my question."

"I'll tell you, I'll tell you!" Thistle said quickly. "Ghorbi took us to the crossroads. We ... traveled from there."

"Ghorbi, eh," Augusta said, and twisted his collar a little.

Thistle nodded in reply.

"So if I go to this 'crossroads,' I can go to the Gardens from there?"

"I reckon so, my lady," Thistle replied.

"And how does one go to the crossroads?" Augusta tightened her grip.

"One sings a song," Thistle wheezed. "I can't breathe."

Augusta let him go. "You will teach me this song."

Thistle straightened and rubbed his throat. He paused and swallowed. Then he said, "I propose a trade, my lady. You have something I need. I have something you need."

Augusta laughed. "Your name, isn't it. Did you come all the way here for your name, boy?"

"I did."

Augusta couldn't help but be impressed. "Very tenacious. And so you thought I'd give it to you."

"As a trade, my lady. It's all I have left."

Augusta looked him up and down. The boy was trembling and wide-eyed. "Very well," she said. "I suppose it's a fair trade." She emptied her glass. "Teach me, and you'll earn your name back."

Thistle held out his hand. "Your word," he said.

Augusta laughed. "Of course." She grabbed his hand and held it just tight enough to feel the bones shift. "You have my word that once you have taught me the song to get to the crossroads, you will have your name back."

Thistle nodded. "We should probably go outside."

"You first," Augusta said. She put her carving knife in her belt, just in case.

The sky had cleared. A faint multicolored aurora glimmered to the north.

"Go on," Augusta said. "Sing."

Thistle started humming. Augusta hummed with him. The sound gradually built into a simple tune, but something that Thistle did made it sound like he was harmonizing with himself. Augusta moved her tongue around in her mouth and adjusted the muscles in her jaw, until she felt a second note reverberate through her skull. Thistle sang a long, long word, and Augusta mimicked him. The song rose and fell, rose and fell. Then Thistle abruptly went quiet.

"There it is," he said. "The crossroads."

Ahead of them, where the mountainside should be, was a blur. The snowy ground at Augusta's feet gradually flattened out and faded into cracked mud.

"You go in, and there are people who will show you the way," Thistle said.

"Excellent, boy. Well done." Augusta started walking.

Thistle grabbed her sleeve. "You gave me your word. My name."

Augusta turned around and looked down at him. "Your name. Of course."

She grabbed his jaw with one hand and looked deep into his eyes. "Albin," she said. "Albin Jönsson is your name."

The boy's eyes filled with tears. He let out a long sigh.

"That means you are completely free," Augusta said. "Which also means I am free to kill you."

Before the boy could react, she snatched the carving knife from her belt and drove it into his stomach.

"Thank you for your service, darling," Augusta said. "Your death will be slow."

She let him go, and he sank to the ground with a groan. Augusta turned around and walked into the haze.

25

When Dora woke up, the room was empty, with only embers glowing in the fireplace. It was quiet save for the faint sound of Stjärna's bell upstairs.

The coveralls she had hung on the back of a chair were gone, replaced by a shift and a woolen skirt and jacket that looked much like Grandmother's. She put them on; they were almost her size, although the jacket was short in the sleeves.

A loaf of bread wrapped in linen sat on the table, together with the box of butter. Dora cut herself a thick slice of bread and chewed on it while she walked up the tunnel to the barn. Grandmother was milking the cows with a rhythmic drizzle; she crooned a slow melody, full of trills and strange consonants, so melancholy it made Dora's heart catch: Lilltåa, tåtilla, kroknosa, tillerosa.

"Why is it so sad?"

Grandmother stopped singing and looked up at her. "It's not sad. It's how we sing." She smiled. "It's a children's song. Counting the toes on your foot. I sang it to our daughter."

"Where is she now?"

Grandmother's smile tightened. She patted the cow's flank. "She snuck down to the village for the Midsummer dance, and a man threw a pair of iron shears over her head. He saw her tail and knew that cold iron would trap her."

She stood up and poured the contents of the bucket into a large crock, then put a lid on it.

"Take the other handle," she said. "We'll put it outside to cool down."

"I would like to go now, please," Dora said.

"We will," Grandmother said. "But the cows need attention."

"What do you do with the milk?" Dora asked.

"We keep some; we give some away to our cousins," Grandmother replied. "There are more of us living here in the mountains."

Outside, the snowy landscape was dazzling in the sunlight. Grandfather was chopping wood on a block next to the cave opening. He nodded at Dora and Grandmother as they carried the crock to a snowdrift. Grandfather put the ax down.

"Is it time?" he asked.

"It is," Grandmother replied.

She patted Dora's shoulder. "Let's get you something to travel in. Shoes, for one."

"No shoes," Dora said. "I don't like shoes."

Grandmother looked at Dora's feet and pursed her lips. "Let me at least give you a shawl. For my own peace of mind."

She went down into the cave. She must have been prepared, because it was only a moment later that she emerged with a birch-bark knapsack and a triangular shawl which she laid over Dora's shoulders, then crossed over her chest and tied at the small of her back. Grandmother tied another shawl over her own shoulders and shouldered the knapsack. Grandfather put on a long mole-skin coat.

"Let's get the skis, then," he said.

"What are skis?" Dora asked.

Grandmother and Grandfather exchanged glances.

"I'll fetch the snowshoes," Grandfather muttered.

It took some time to get used to the woven frames that Grand-father strapped to Dora's feet. After a while, she could let herself sink into the rhythm of the wide-legged walk. She listened to the creak of snow under their feet, the rustle of fabric, the steady breaths, sometimes syncopated by an animal shrieking about its territory. Some of the gnawing fear dissipated. Worrying about Thistle on the way was pointless.

They plodded down into the valley, through the pine forest, and up the other side where the mountain lay bare between tufts of old grass and heather. They went through the pass and down into the next valley. On the way, Grandmother sung something in a dialect Dora didn't understand but whose notes, at once sad and joyous, sent shivers down her arms.

"I don't suppose you ever learned the songs of your people?" Grandmother asked in the silence that followed.

"No," Dora replied. "I don't know if I have a people. My father abandoned me."

"Perhaps your mother, then?"

"I don't know if I have a mother," Dora said. "I came from the earth."

"Then the earth is your mother," Grandmother said, "and that's a good mother to have."

She pointed north. "The most lovely music I have heard is that by our saajvoe cousins. They don't quite sing like we do; they jojk." The word was soft and wistful in her mouth.

"You don't jojk *about* animals or moods or the sun over the mountains. Do you see? The song is the thing. A fox jojk is the fox. A happiness jojk is happiness."

"I want to hear it," Dora said. "Can you do it?"

Grandmother shook her head. "I would never presume to. That song belongs to the saajvoe. Perhaps you will meet them one day."

They passed the silent rockslide and walked down into the next valley. In the last light from the sun, a farm came into view. Sounds came from inside the barn. As Dora drew closer, she saw that the yard in front of the house was stained crimson. A trail led from the yard and up the stairs to the front door.

"Odd," Grandmother said.

"I'll check on the animals," said Grandfather.

"Good," Grandmother said. "Dora, with me."

Grandmother walked up to the front door of the house and banged on it three times.

"Nils! It's Grandmother come to visit."

There was no reply. Grandmother opened the door.

The thick smell of blood shoved itself into Dora's nose.

"Nils?" Grandmother called, and went into the kitchen.

"Oh dear," she said from inside.

Dora stepped into the kitchen with her.

Thistle was curled up on the kitchen bench. Dora couldn't

tell if he was breathing. She shoved past Grandmother and knelt down next to him. She brushed stray locks out of his face. He groaned. He was breathing, but just barely. Grandmother set her satchel down and knelt next to Dora.

"Help me turn him on his back," Grandmother said.

Thistle's eyelids fluttered; he let out a high whimper. The whole front of his shirt and trousers were stiff with gore. Grandmother lifted Thistle's hands from his belly. It was such a little wound to make so much blood come out.

"Thistle?" Dora said. "Thistle."

Thistle's eyes opened very wide.

"You were dead," he said in a hoarse whisper.

Dora shook her head. "I'm sorry I took so long. I feel asleep."

Thistle's mouth trembled. "You . . . fell asleep."

"I'm so sorry," Dora said, and buried her face in his hair.

"Grandmother will take care of you now," she said.

Thistle's eyes went from Dora to Grandmother, who was rummaging in her backpack.

"Who is she?"

"She's a good person," Dora said. "She'll help you."

"Don't let her hurt me."

"I won't," Dora said.

She held Thistle as Grandmother cleaned his wound.

"It's deep," she said. "We'll need good magic for this." She pointed to a bucket on the floor. "Go outside and fill this with snow."

When Dora came back inside, Grandmother had stoked a fire in the stove and was mashing something with a mortar and pestle. She pointed at Dora to set the bucket down next to the stove, and scooped some snow out of it into a copper pot.

"Dora," Thistle whispered from the kitchen bench.

Dora knelt down next to him. He was shivering. She sat down on the floor next to the sofa and cradled his face in her hands. He had a beard, now, scraggly and redder than his hair. His forehead was very cold. He stared back at her, and his eyes were wild.

"He said you were dead," Thistle said again. "But it wasn't him. It was Augusta."

Dora shook her head. "I don't understand."

"He was Augusta in disguise," Thistle said. "It was her. And she kept me here. Told me you were dead. I grieved. I gave up."

"But I'm not," Dora said. "I'm not. I was a stone."

Thistle frowned. "What?"

Dora shrugged. "I was a stone. Where is she?"

"Gone," Thistle said. "Gone."

He closed his eyes and seemed to fall asleep.

"Thistle," Dora said, and shook his shoulder.

"That's not my name," he mumbled.

Grandmother came over to the kitchen bench, mortar in her hands. She knelt down next to the sofa.

"This will hurt, my dear," she told Thistle. "Dora, hold his hands."

Dora held on as Grandmother scooped sharp-smelling goop out of the mortar and packed it into Thistle's wound. Thistle didn't scream but went stiff and started to shiver violently. Grandmother covered the poultice with a strip of cotton and bound it tight around his waist. Then she laid a hand on the poultice and started to sing. It was a low, muted song that wound in circles and spirals, in that dialect that Dora didn't understand. Thistle's arms gradually relaxed.

"There," Grandmother said. "That'll draw the bad fluids out and heal the wound."

Thistle's face had gone from sickly to slightly rosy, and he seemed to breathe easier. Grandmother nodded to herself.

"He'll be all right in a while," she said.

The front door opened, and there was a stomping and scraping noise as Grandfather kicked snow from his boots. He came into the kitchen and exchanged glances with Grandmother.

"The cows were alone in there for a while," he said. "I had to milk them. There's a horse, too. I don't know whose it is."

"Nils is gone," Grandmother said. "It seems he hurt this boy badly."

"He said it wasn't Nils," Dora said. "He said it was Augusta."

Grandfather frowned.

"Not now," Grandmother said. "We'll need to take this boy home."

26

Thistle wasn't light anymore; he had put on muscle. But Dora carried him all the way back to the mine, through the night lit by Grandmother and Grandfather's lanterns. They brought the horse and the cows, too; the animals followed without protest. Then Dora bedded Thistle down by the fireplace and let him sleep. She sat on the floor next to him, watching. She shook her head when Grandfather asked if she wasn't going to rest. She had had enough sleep. While Grandfather and Grandmother went to bed, Dora sank back, letting her breathing slow down, concentrating on Thistle's right hand in hers. It had calluses now, and dirt under the fingernails. He would need a bath. He had always been so mindful about bathing.

Grandmother and Grandfather got up again after what seemed like no time at all, and Grandmother checked on Thistle's wound and said it looked all right. Then she asked Dora to help her with breakfast while Grandfather went to take care of the cows. They moved Thistle into the armchair by the fire. Dora sat down next to him and spooned buttered porridge into his mouth, because his hands were shaking so much he couldn't feed himself. He was still clammy and sickly-looking, but his eyes had lost the crazed gleam of the day before. He didn't speak until the bowl was empty.

"I was supposed to take care of you," he said, and his voice was creaky. "Not the other way around."

"Not in the outside world," Dora said. "You taught me how to live in the Gardens. Now I'll protect you here."

"I mourned you. I missed you so much," he said, and his voice broke.

Dora took his hand. "I'm here now," she said.

Thistle held out his arm, and she lifted him into her lap. He rested his head on her shoulder, breathing in deep sighs. Dora smoothed down his hair and kissed the top of his head.

"It was Augusta," Thistle said into her shoulder. "It was her the whole time. She made me teach her the song to the crossroads. But I got my name back."

"What's your name?" Dora asked.

"Albin," he mumbled. "It's Albin."

"It's a good name," Dora said.

"I remember everything now," he said. "When she gave me my name . . . it all came back. My parents, who they are. My village. Where it is. I know the way now."

He raised his head, casting a glance around the room. Grandmother stood in the doorway. She gave Albin a gentle smile.

"I could tell you to trust us, but that wouldn't reassure you," she said.

"I'll watch over you," Dora told Albin. "Until you're healed."

Albin looked at Grandmother, then Dora.

"Only until I'm better," he said.

Dora nodded. "Only until you're better."

They stayed with Grandmother and Grandfather while the days shortened and snow piled up around the mine's entrance. Dora helped Grandmother and Grandfather with the last preparations for a long winter; Grandfather taught her to ski and snare grouse. One day Albin stepped out of the mine, and soon enough he too had his first go at skiing. He talked more and smiled again. Sometimes he would talk about his parents, but hesitantly, as if the memories would break when he spoke them out loud: *My father taught me how to whittle wood. My mother has eyes like that. We had an apple tree and a dog.*

He would let only Dora come near him. If their hosts took offense, they didn't show it.

One evening, Albin sat down beside Dora where she was peeling potatoes next to Grandmother.

"I'm ready," he said. "I want to go home."

Dora looked at him. Albin reached out and rubbed his thumb over Dora's cheek.

"You still manage to get dirt everywhere," he said with a grin.

Dora smiled back at him.

Albin's smile softened a little. "You've changed, though."

"How?"

"I can't put my finger on it." He leaned back. "You seem happier. Like you belong here."

"Do you know where you're going, then?" Grandmother asked.

"We're following my name," Albin said. "I can feel it calling me. Home. Where I came from. I know the way now. It's south."

⟶

Grandmother and Grandfather wouldn't let them leave without a birch-bark satchel each, stuffed with food and with a woolen blanket on top.

"Off you go, then," Grandfather said, and his voice was thick.

"Good luck," Grandmother added.

Grandfather gave Dora a tight hug, then held his arms out to Albin, who blinked and offered his hand instead. Grandmother put her arms around Dora. She seemed smaller somehow.

"Goodbye, daughter of the earth," she said as she drew away. "You remind me of my own."

She and Grandfather joined hands and walked back into the mine.

They started out when it was still dark; dawn trickled into the sky as they strapped their skis on. The air crackled with cold.

Albin pushed himself down the hill. Dora followed in his wake.

PART IV

HOMECOMING

27

Augusta walked to the enclosure in the middle of the burnt plain. Her eyes still stung from the wind that had whipped at her as she passed from the hillside into this eerie landscape. The sky had taken on a sickly shade; in its center shone a dark disc surrounded by a bright halo. So this was the crossroads.

She looked at her hands. They were still Nils Nilsson's hands, an old man's hands, coarse from work. She could feel this body weigh on her, an ill-fitting suit made of flesh. *You will be Nils Nilsson forever or until one of your own recognizes and names you.* Thistle knew, but he was beneath her. He wasn't one of her own.

The creatures swaddled in lengths of ashen fabric looked very busy at their tables. She tapped the nearest one on the shoulder. It looked up from the orb it was fiddling with.

"You," she said. "I need to go to the Gardens."

The creature tilted its head and regarded her with enormous eyes that didn't have proper pupils. It seemed completely hairless, its skin shiny and artificial-looking. A clucking sound came out through its little slit of a mouth.

"The Gardens," Augusta repeated. "Show me to the Gardens. Now."

The creature rubbed its fingers together and closed its eyes. Then it opened them again and pointed to Augusta's right, across the plain.

"There's nothing there," Augusta said.

It snapped its fingers and pointed again. It said something in that clucking voice.

"Right," Augusta said. "I'll walk."

The ground changed first. Blades of grass shot up in the cracks between the mud plates, then grew into saplings. Shadows wavered in front of Augusta, and she stepped in among them, and they coalesced into tall beech trees. She was walking in a forest. Patches of daylight danced across the path before her. In the distance, the buzz of voices. Something felt off. The trees weren't birches, and the daylight wasn't supposed to be there, and there was no dancing rhythm. Still, Augusta walked on.

The trees gave way to a clearing, a hollow in the landscape. A tall, spindly tower rose up against a cerulean sky; around it milled shapes dressed in identical hooded cloaks. Augusta couldn't see their faces. The buzz of voices was louder.

When Augusta approached, the crowd parted before her but didn't otherwise acknowledge her presence. The hoods on their cloaks obscured their features entirely. She couldn't hear anyone speak, but the faraway voices didn't recede. It was as if people were talking around her but not close to her. She reached out at random and grabbed a shoulder. The figure whirled around.

"You," Augusta said. "Where am I?"

The figure stood very still. Augusta tried to peek inside its hood, but the figure was shorter than her and the hood hung very low.

"Show your face," she said.

The figure remained impassive. Augusta lifted the edge of its hood. The buzz became louder.

Where there should have been a face was a blank surface across which little points of light danced in shapes too quick to follow. A mumble emanated from that surface. Augusta leaned closer to listen.

"Three, nine, seven, one, five," a woman's voice intoned. "Three, nine, seven, one, five."

The voice was replaced by a loud, artificial-sounding tune. Augusta flinched and dropped the edge of the hood she had been holding.

"Three, nine, seven, one, five," the figure said.

Augusta let go and took a step backward. She bumped into something. She turned around and was met by another figure, so tall that she was staring right up into its hood. There was that same blank space of a face. It emitted a cheerful, plinking tune.

Augusta shied away from the figure only to crash into someone else, and someone else again. She pushed through the crowd, past bleeping noises and recited numbers, and reached the trees. The beings didn't seem to have taken any notice whatsoever. The tall spire gleamed.

She must have been sent to the wrong place. Augusta took a deep breath and sang the song.

The crossroads looked exactly the same. Augusta approached the nearest creature she could find. Perhaps it was the same one who had pointed her to that place with the tower; perhaps not.

"The Gardens," Augusta said. "I was supposed to go to the Gardens, but you pointed me in the wrong direction."

It did that head-tilting motion, then pointed, very decisively, to Augusta's left.

"Fine," Augusta said, and headed that way.

Augusta arrived at a labyrinthine garden the size of a city and went back to the crossroads. She was pointed to a garden of taxidermied animals. Then a garden with sculptures carved from ice. She came to a garden of living trees and ate screaming fruit that tasted of spices and flesh. She did not sleep there, although the ground was soft and inviting. None of these were her Gardens. Rage grew in her chest.

The eighth time she came back to the crossroads, she marched up to a booth and stared down at the creature seated there.

"You know where I need to go," she said between her teeth. "You just won't take me there."

It looked up at her and clucked its tongue. It raised a hand to vaguely point at a spot behind her.

"No," Augusta said. "No more."

She gripped the miserable thing by its throat and squeezed. Its neck was frail, the skin dry and scratchy. She could feel the rest of them crowding around her, chattering, tearing at her clothes, but they were not nearly as strong as her. She snapped the creature's neck. The others let go of her and fell silent. Augusta turned around.

"Do as I tell you!" she roared.

Later, Augusta sat down with her back to the enclosure just to rest for a little while. Behind her, tables were overturned and little bodies littered the ground. No one had been helpful. They had paid for it.

"There you are," a familiar voice said.

Augusta looked up. A tall shape wrapped in shadowy silks loomed over her.

"Ghorbi," Augusta said.

Ghorbi said nothing, just looked at her. Augusta got to her feet and took a step backward. She still had to crane her neck to meet Ghorbi's eyes.

Ghorbi looked her up and down. "I know who you are, Augusta."

Augusta brightened. "You know me!"

She waited for something to happen. Nothing did. Of course. Ghorbi was not one of her own.

She sighed. "I'm stuck in some old man's body."

"Indeed," Ghorbi replied, then paused. "I came here on business. This is not what I expected to see."

"They refused to help me," Augusta muttered.

"Do you know what you have done, Augusta?" Ghorbi said.

Augusta shrugged. "Punished them."

Ghorbi let out something between a guffaw and a growl, then

bent over Augusta. "This place is a hub in the multiverse. And only these folk know the directions. You have just made travel between worlds impossible to almost everyone, you idiot."

Ghorbi stepped around Augusta, who made to follow her. Ghorbi held up a hand. Her voice was tense with suppressed wrath.

"You will stay where you are."

Ghorbi walked around between the bodies, checking each one for signs of life.

"Ah," she mumbled, and helped one of them into a sitting position.

Augusta closed her eyes and heard Ghorbi whisper to the creature in its own language. All this action had depleted her, and her knuckles hurt.

After a while, she heard footsteps approach again and looked up. Ghorbi loomed over her.

"One of them is still alive," she said. "Fortunately. The crossroads is still functional."

"I just want to go home," Augusta said. "I'm tired."

"I don't kill," Ghorbi said. "I made a vow long ago to follow a god that will not allow it. But I will take you back to your Gardens. You will do less damage there."

Ghorbi started walking in a direction that was ever so slightly different from the one Augusta had taken last. She stopped and motioned ahead of her.

"Go on," Ghorbi said. "Go. Before I change my mind about my vow."

28

Dora and Albin traveled south between the mountains. They rested under trees or in the occasional empty barn along the way, getting up at dawn to move on south while the short day lasted. Dora relished the deep silence of the snowy mountains, the exhilaration of going downhill into a valley, even the slog of putting on ski skins and climbing up the other side. Her body seemed built for it. Albin was doing all right, too; he had turned rosy, and his beard had thickened. He smiled more often than not. He was the one who got up first in the mornings, eager to move on. He spoke about his family along the way: his affable father who made furniture and took Albin on fishing trips; his quiet mother who sewed dresses for fancy ladies and made him help her in the kitchen. He couldn't wait to see them. They would be older now, but not terribly old. Perhaps there would be younger siblings.

One day they crested a hill and came into a valley where the snow had been broken up by rain. They left their skis in an unused sheep shelter and continued on foot.

"We're getting closer," Albin said. "I can feel it. What if they don't recognize me?"

His smile had vanished. Dora put an arm around him.

"I'm here," she said. "I'm with you."

Albin looked up at her. "I wouldn't be here otherwise."

He tugged his cap down around his ears and continued into the valley, where tall pines swallowed the daylight. Mossy boulders lay strewn about on the ground.

Albin pointed at a particularly large rock. "My mother said they were thrown here by giants," he said, and smiled.

Patches of snow lingered in the hollows at their base.

"This is so familiar," Albin said. "I think I used to hide here."

He walked ahead of Dora, at first hesitant, then more confident. An aspen tree broke the monotony of pine. Then another. As pine gradually gave way to deciduous forest, the air grew damp. An overcast sky became visible through the branches. The ground was soggy with melting snow.

In the evening they came to a wall made of piled-up stones. On the other side ran a trail. Albin climbed over the stones and started walking down it. In not too long, they saw a cluster of small wooden houses with white corners that almost shone in the murk.

"There were two apple trees in the yard," Albin said to himself.

They walked down the trail, past houses with empty windows, with buckling porches and ruined front steps. Debris lay here and there in the yards, humps with sharp edges.

"Where is everyone?" Dora wondered.

"Maybe they're all in the fields or at church," Albin said, but he didn't sound convinced.

He suddenly stopped.

"There," he said. "There it is."

The two-story house was slightly larger than the others. It had a small sagging porch, on which stood a bench and a bucket. The two enormous apple trees that flanked the path up to the house were gnarled and unkempt. From one of them hung two tattered ropes.

"My father put that swing up for me," Albin whispered.

"Are you going to knock?" Dora said.

Albin remained where he was. "It looks different," he said. "And like no one's home." His lower lip trembled. "I don't know if I can do this."

"I'll go," Dora said.

She went up the path and stepped onto the porch, which complained under her weight. Nothing moved inside. Dora knocked on the door. When no one came to open it, she tried the handle. The door was locked. Dora looked over her shoulder. Albin hadn't moved: he stood in a puddle on the path, his face wan in the weakening light. Dora pulled at the handle, hard. The door came off its hinges. She caught it and propped it up against the wall.

The hall beyond was empty and smelled of mildew and dust. Dora heard Albin's footsteps behind her, then his gasp. He went past her and walked into a room on the right.

"Mamma?" he called from in there. "Pappa?"

His footsteps moved away, up a set of stairs. His voice called out, over and over. Then silence.

Dora followed. Nothing stirred inside the house. The little corpses of flies and spiders rested on the windowsills. She found Albin in a room on the second floor. He was sitting in a small alcove, head in his hands.

"They're gone," he said. "They left without me."

Dora said nothing, just sat down next to him and held him as he cried. Eventually, he fell asleep. Then she laid him down and went downstairs. The chill had deepened outside; the puddles on the ground were icing over. Dora's breath came out in great clouds. The cloud cover broke, and a few stars came out. Dora stood there, listening to the noise of puddles freezing and birds rustling in the forest, until the crows woke up and lights came on in the house farthest down the road.

Albin came outside. He looked shivery in the open air. Dora wrapped her arms around him from behind to warm him up.

"Look," she said. "Someone's there." She pointed to the little house where the lights were turned on.

The man who opened the door was very old. He looked at Dora and Albin in surprise.

"Who might you be, then?" he said.

"My name is Albin," Albin said. "I used to live here. I'm looking for my parents."

"Very well," the man said. "My name is Börje. Come in, won't you?" he added, like it was the most natural thing in the world.

Börje showed them into his kitchen and boiled a brew of ground seeds and water at the stove. Dora and Albin sat in silence while he poured them each a cup.

"Now, then," he said. "Tell me what you're doing out here."

"My parents," Albin said. "Edvin and Amanda. They're not here. Where are they?"

"Edvin and Amanda Jönsson?" the old man asked.

Albin nodded. "I came back to look for them. They're not there. The house . . ." His breath caught. "The house is empty."

Börje was quiet for a long moment. He looked at Albin, then at Dora, and seemed to make a decision.

"There was a boy," he said. "The Jönsson boy. He disappeared. The whole village looked for him. His mamma swore that he had been taken by the fair folk. Of course, no one believed her. They all said that he must have gotten lost in the forest or drowned somewhere, or wolves took him." He peered at Albin. "You're that boy, aren't you."

Albin nodded. He sat on the edge of his chair, eyes brimming.

The old man sucked at his front teeth and sipped from his cup. "So it's true then."

"Where are they?" Albin asked.

"This all happened when I was little," Börje replied. "My mamma and pappa told me about it. They never let me go into the forest on my own."

"Where are my parents?" Albin repeated.

Börje put his hand on Albin's. "They're gone. They died many years ago. I'm sorry."

Albin stared at his cup.

"How many years?" he said eventually. "Since I left."

"Oh," the man said. "I'm eighty-five. I'm the last one here in the village. Everyone moved to the city when the foundry closed down. Maybe they'll come back if the war comes here. But for now, it's just me."

"The war?" Dora asked.

"Yes. There's a war on. There's an evil man who wants to conquer the world. He has occupied our brother nations to the west and south. But he's not here yet."

"But what if he does come?" Dora said.

"Then we do what we can to survive," he replied. "Most people are good at heart. We will help each other. And if people come here to hide, well, I will help them."

"I don't care about the war!" Albin shouted. "I want my mamma and pappa."

"I'm so sorry, Albin," Börje said, and his voice was soft. "They never forgot about you."

Börje walked them down to an old church not far from the village. It seemed disused, its doors barred. The graves in the yard outside were ordered in neat rows. No flowers adorned the graves; the grass that stuck up through the rotten snow had grown wild.

"Here we are," Börje said. "Now let's find your parents."

The gravestone was tucked in a corner beneath a birch. EDVIN JÖNSSON 1825–1898, it said, AND HIS WIFE AMANDA 1828–1902. THEIR SON ALBIN, MISSED AND LOVED. Lichen dotted the stone and crept up its sides. Albin crouched down in front of the stone. He said nothing, just cried. Dora waited and listened to the magpies arguing with each other in the tree. Börje stood next to her, hands clasped behind his back.

Finally, Albin stood up and turned to face them. His eyes were swollen and his jaw was set.

"There is nothing for me here," he said.

"What will you do?" Börje asked.

"Go elsewhere," Albin replied. "We have something to do."

"Very well," Börje said. "Is there anything I can do to help?"

Albin shook his head. "No. You have already helped."

Börje nodded. "I suppose I will leave you to it. Be well, Albin Jönsson."

He shook hands with Dora and Albin, and then wandered back up the slope toward the village.

When he was out of sight, Dora asked, "What exactly is it we have to do?"

"Find Augusta again," Albin said. "And kill her."

"It didn't go so well last time," Dora said.

"I wasn't who I am now," Albin replied. "I can do it. I don't have to fight her. I just need the Memory Theater to help us. I have a plan."

"What's the plan?"

"They tell memories. Maybe they'll tell a new memory."

Albin began to sing.

29

Slender birch trees sprung up around Augusta as she walked. There was a familiar scent in the air: apples. The sky changed into the familiar hue of a summer night. The grass was thick under her feet. Augusta looked at her hands: still worn and square. Not her own. But these woods were familiar. Here and there, things hung on the lower tree branches: a glass prism on a string, a strip of silk, a bird skull in a silver net. They formed a path deeper in between the trees.

The splash of water made Augusta turn her head. Not too far away, a pond she recognized.

"Hello," a voice said.

A heart-shaped face framed by blond locks peered at Augusta from under a small overhang. The face smiled, and its teeth were pointed.

Porla tilted her head. "Who is this gentleman?"

Augusta blinked. "Porla?"

Porla let out a tinkling laugh. "The gentleman knows! I am honored. Welcome to my home. Would my lord like to see it? I have a friend I could introduce. Who are you? Are you lost?" She squinted at Augusta, then said, "I know you. Don't I?"

Augusta's eyes prickled. Something that had been clenched in her chest let go in a sobbing sigh. Porla came out from under the overhang and reached for Augusta's ankle. Her skin was flecked like a frog's, her touch icy.

"You know me," Augusta whispered. "By what name do you know me?"

Porla pawed at Augusta's leg and stared up into her eyes. "It's on the tip of my tongue." Then she paused, and her eyes drifted down to the water.

Then she looked up again. "I can introduce you to my friend."

"Do you recognize me? Say my name," Augusta said.

Porla smiled with her needle teeth and shook her head. "The tip of my tongue," she said.

Augusta felt her heart sink.

"Let me show you my friend," Porla said. "That will make you happy."

Augusta shook her leg free of Porla's hand. "I'm not interested in your friend, Porla."

Porla's lower lip quivered. "No one ever is," she said.

"Good," Augusta said.

She looked back as she walked away. Porla was under the overhang again, arms around what looked like a bloated body. Porla whispered to it intently and glared at Augusta. Then she dived under the surface and dragged the corpse down with her.

⁓

There was a drumbeat, uneven and heavy. Little lanterns were strung from the branches. In the distance, the flash of colorful silks moving in time to the music. Augusta peeked from behind a tree. They were dancing in slow graceful movements, their powdered faces shining in the dusk. Augusta swayed to the rhythm. She could burst onto the marble floor now, join them in the dance. But would they know her in this guise? Would they say, "Ah, Augusta, we see you"? Porla didn't. Would they murder her as an invader?

The music ended. The lady Mnemosyne's voice filled the air.

"A game," she called. "We shall have a game."

A cheer went up, and the dancers formed a line. Mnemosyne led the way out of the statuary grove and toward the game lawn. Augusta followed them at a distance.

"Stop right there," a voice said.

Augusta turned around to see Walpurgis a few steps behind her. He was poised like a statue in his elaborate dress, corkscrew locks in a perfect frame around his exquisite visage. He held a hand up in a forbidding gesture.

"You don't belong here," he said.

"Do you not know me?" Augusta said.

She had to make Walpurgis name her.

"You do not look like anyone I know," Walpurgis replied. He took a step closer. "But I will concede that there is something familiar about you."

"I am trapped in someone else's flesh," Augusta said. "It follows me around wherever I go."

"Interesting," Walpurgis said.

He closed in and inspected her with heavy-lidded eyes. His breath was thick with wine.

"Do I know you?" he said. "Do I?"

"Please, Walpurgis," Augusta said. "You know me. We have danced together in the Gardens, so many times, so many nights."

"There is only tonight," Walpurgis said, and cocked his head.

"I know," Augusta said. "Again and again. And during all those agains, we have danced. My hair is curled mahogany; my eyes are dove gray; I wear a coat the shade of the sky. But I am stuck in this other body. I need you to let me out. Say my name."

"Your name?" Walpurgis repeated. "There is a lord . . . isn't there?"

"Not a lord," Augusta replied. "Me."

She grabbed Walpurgis by the collar. "Look at me."

Walpurgis frowned, then sniffed at her. "What's that scent?" he mumbled. "Lily of the valley."

Augusta let out a sob. "Yes. Lily of the valley. Who smells like that?"

Walpurgis looked into her eyes. "Only the lady Augusta smells like that."

"That's right," Augusta said.

Walpurgis looked confused. "Augusta?"

Augusta's stomach clenched. She nodded and let go of his collar. Walpurgis remained where he was, so close that she could see the veins in his eyes.

"We like to play croquet," Walpurgis said. "On the lawn."

Augusta reached out and squeezed his hand. "Say it again. Say my name."

Walpurgis bent his head to sniff at her neck. "Augusta Prima," he said. "Augusta Prima is your name."

As Walpurgis spoke, a shiver went through Augusta. The flesh sheath that held her seemed to loosen its grip a little. She let go of Walpurgis's hand and held her own up to her face. The skin looked translucent somehow, saggy. She could feel her own body underneath, pushing and straining against its prison. She flung her hands back and tore at the fabric between her shoulder blades. The fabric tore, and the shirt underneath, and the skin underneath.

It was not quite as easy as taking off a suit. Walpurgis watched in silence as Augusta struggled her way out of Nils Nilsson's body. Eventually, she stood naked on the forest floor, the other body at her feet.

Augusta looked down at herself. She was herself again, a woman in her prime, albeit bloody and naked as a newborn baby. The relief made her burst into laughter.

"Thank you, Walpurgis," she said. "Do you see me now?"

"I see you," Walpurgis said. "Augusta."

"Good," Augusta replied. "Take me to the others."

Walpurgis bowed and walked ahead of her to the game lawn.

Here they were: Euterpe naked among the bushes, Virgilia and Cymbeline embracing a servant, Tempestis and the other courtiers dancing with their croquet clubs, swinging in time to the ever-present beat. They were all here.

"I'm here!" Augusta said to no one in particular.

Euterpe came running with a wide smile.

"Sister," she said. "You're naked! And extravagantly soiled!"

Augusta laughed. "So I am."

"How delightful," Euterpe said.

Augusta embraced her sister. Her eyes watered a little. She caressed Euterpe's face, and got a frown in response.

"What's that, crying? We can't have that. Let's find you something to wear."

"And a bath," Augusta said. "I need a bath."

Euterpe had a servant fetch a bucket of water, and everyone gathered around Augusta to watch as she cleaned herself of the blood. When Augusta was done and had dried herself off, Euterpe pointed to a servant at the edge of the lawn. He gave her a frightened look and started to back away.

"You. Undress," Augusta told him. "Give your clothes to me."

The servant's trousers and vest fit Augusta unexpectedly well. She borrowed Euterpe's discarded silk jacket, and lo: she was once again dressed for a party.

Augusta made a twirl, and there was Mnemosyne on her throne. She had been watching the whole time. Augusta walked up to the dais and bowed.

"My lady," she said, "I am here."

"So you are," Mnemosyne said, face unreadable under her laurel wreath. Her eyes were clouded. She opened her mouth, then closed it again. Then she said, "I cast you out."

Augusta swallowed. "Did you, my lady?"

"I . . ." Mnemosyne faltered. "Did I not?"

"Not me," Augusta said. "Never me. See? I am beautiful and young. I live only to please you. I can do a little dance? Sing a little song? Would that please my lady?"

"There is something," Mnemosyne mumbled. "I forget."

"There is nothing," Augusta said. She could feel a trickle of sweat between her shoulder blades. "Nothing at all."

"You seem troubled," Mnemosyne said, and raised her glass. "Here. Drink and be happy."

The wine was acidic on Augusta's tongue, but she emptied the glass.

"Good," Mnemosyne said. "Go play."

She sagged back in her throne, and for a moment she looked very old. Augusta left the dais and held out a hand. A servant appeared with a glass of wine. It tasted sweeter. The third glass was exquisite. Out on the lawn, the others danced in a circle. The circle dispersed, and the lords and ladies picked up their croquet clubs. Things began to soften at the edges.

30

"Something's wrong," Albin said as they approached the enclosure at the crossroads. "It's too quiet."

He was right. There was no distant noise of commerce or murmur of voices. The halo in the sky cast an eerie light on the landscape.

"Maybe they're asleep," Dora said.

It was only when they came through the gap in the low wall that they saw the corpses. They were laid out in a neat line between the tables, their faces covered by cloth. Stains spread across the front of some of them; limbs stuck out at odd angles, as if broken.

Next to Dora, Albin let out a little shriek. Dora instinctively put an arm around him and held him close.

"I'm going to have a look," Dora said. "Stay here."

Albin gave a quick nod.

Dora edged her way around the bodies. There was no smell,

even though the air was still. She could hear a rustling sound nearby and approached it.

On the far side of the enclosure, Ghorbi was digging a shallow ditch. She had rolled her sleeves up to her elbows and gripped a shovel that looked too small for the job. When Dora came closer, she straightened. Her eyes burned with suppressed rage.

"Hello again," she said. "Sorry about the mess."

"What happened?" Dora asked.

Ghorbi dropped the shovel and gestured at the scene. "Augusta happened."

"Oh," Dora said.

"Augusta?" Albin said behind her. He had followed her without her noticing.

Ghorbi pointed at a creature sitting with its back against the wall. "Happily, she left one alive. The crossroads will recover, eventually."

"Where is she?" Albin asked. "Augusta."

"I pointed her to the Gardens," Ghorbi replied. "She was wreaking havoc."

Albin took Dora's hand. "We have to go. Ghorbi, where is the Memory Theater?"

Ghorbi looked at the ditch. "I have places to be, too. But this has to be done. I can't leave them like this."

"I'm good at digging pits," Dora offered. "Let me."

"We don't have time!" Albin said.

"If she managed to get back in, she isn't going anywhere," Ghorbi replied. "Show some respect for the dead."

Dora took off her jacket and shawl, hiked up her skirt around her waist, and dug a long pit that would fit the eleven bodies on the ground. The soil listened to her and parted for her. Ghorbi spoke to the survivor in hushed tones; Albin sat down next to them, looking slightly ill. When Dora was done, she carried each of the bodies to the pit and gently laid them down. Then she asked the soil for help to cover them, and it did.

"There," she said. "It's done."

Ghorbi helped the remaining traffic controller onto its feet. It ambled into the enclosure, where it began to pick things up off the ground and put them back on their tables.

"Well done," Ghorbi told Dora. "That was an act of kindness."

Albin took one of Dora's grimy hands. Ghorbi looked them up and down, as if seeing them properly for the first time.

"You have come a long way since last I saw you," she said.

"And I have my name," Albin said. "And I found my parents."

"And?"

"I had been gone too long," Albin said, and his eyes were glassy. "They died while I was away."

"I see," Ghorbi said. "I'm sorry."

"We have to get back to the Memory Theater," Dora said. "Albin has a plan."

Albin was tense next to her. "Please tell us where they are."

"I don't know," Ghorbi said. "But I'll ask the traffic controller if it does."

She went over to the traffic controller and bent down to speak to it. It nodded and walked past Dora and Albin onto the plain, leaning on Ghorbi's arm.

About fifty paces from the enclosure, the creature pointed at the ground.

"Is that how we get there?" Albin said.

The creature bowed its head and walked back to whence it came.

"I must leave you," Ghorbi said.

"Will we see you again?" Albin asked.

"Perhaps," Ghorbi replied. "I have interfered as much as I can. I want you to find Augusta. I want you to be well. But there are rules I must follow."

She walked off in a different direction, robes billowing behind her, and was quickly out of sight.

Dora dug into the ground with her hands until she was standing knee-deep in a pit about two paces across.

"Dora," Albin said, "we have to tell them about Apprentice."

Dora looked up at him. "I buried her on the mountain."

"So you told me. We have to tell them."

"Will they be angry?"

"Probably. Are you afraid?"

Dora shook her head. "No."

"I am." Albin gnawed on his left thumb. "I don't know if they're people at all."

"Of course they are," Dora said. "Just not people like us."

"Journeyman fell in love with you."

Dora considered this, then nodded.

"Did you fall in love with him?"

"I feel things about him," Dora said. "I like feeling them."

"So are you nervous about seeing him again?" Albin asked.

"Why?"

"He might be angry."

"Because I buried Apprentice?"

Albin made a frustrated noise. "No, because we have to tell them Apprentice is dead. They might think it's our fault. And they might hurt us. They can do magic. Like the lords and ladies."

"That makes no sense," Dora said. "It's not our fault."

"They might not see it that way."

Dora shrugged. "I can't do anything about that. They'll be angry, or they won't be," she said. "But until you know, there's no use being afraid. And if they're really powerful, then there's nothing we can do. And then there's no use being afraid either. I promise I'll be afraid later if we need to."

Albin chortled, then burst into laughter. Dora smiled back at him. Then Albin hopped down into the pit. The ground gave way under their feet.

31

Dancing. Drinking. Eating. Hunting. The Gardens, a place of eternal youth and beauty. Augusta feasted, slept, dressed herself, feasted, slept. It was not so difficult to forget about mountains, cities, a multitude of other worlds. To forget about wearing someone else's skin, peeling it off like an old glove. Augusta was home. She would never leave.

On the croquet lawn, Mnemosyne clapped her hands three times.

Euterpe walked up to Augusta and handed her a club.

"It's Augusta's turn," she called out.

A polished croquet ball sat in the middle of the lawn. Augusta walked out to it and swung her club. The ball landed on the arm of a page, who doubled over. Everyone else clapped their hands and cheered. The game was afoot.

Augusta watched as the others played. She held out her hand

for more wine. Her head felt blurry. Her vision swam. Perhaps she should have a canapé.

She was startled by a loud crack. Cymbeline and Virgilia had hit Augusta's ball with theirs so hard that it shot into the bushes. The others jeered at Augusta.

"You're out!" Cymbeline called.

Augusta sneered at her and dropped the empty wineglass on the ground.

The others continued the game as Augusta wandered in among the trees to find her ball. Her face was numb with drink. It was difficult to see details in the shrubbery. Augusta pushed her way out of a dog-rose bush, and there it was: the ball, sitting next to the corpse of an old man.

Augusta crept closer. The man was old and hoary, his hands large and callused, his face contorted in a silent scream. He looked familiar somehow, but Augusta couldn't quite place him. Why would he be so familiar? And what had brought him here? Only children ever ventured into the woods by mistake. A gold chain trailed from one of his pockets. Augusta bent forward, grasped the chain, and gave it a tug. A shiny locket emerged on the end of the chain, engraved with flowers. Augusta swung the locket up in the air and let it land in her palm. The touch sent a little chill along her arm, and for a moment she felt faint. She wrapped the locket in a handkerchief she found in the sleeve on her shirt, put it in a pocket, and returned to the croquet lawn. Never mind the corpse. She had to win the game.

There was a rustle in the undergrowth as she made her way back to the lawn. Augusta turned around; a shadow receded behind a tree. Had she seen a pair of yellow eyes? She shook her head. No. Silly. There were only the lords and ladies in this place.

❖

Augusta lay on her side in her bed, the little locket resting in her hand. It popped open when she pressed a button on the side, and closed with a sweet little click. She wanted to lick it and eat it and crush it at the same time. There was something wonderful about it and something very bad. She wasn't sure what. But pages knew these things. They had seen the world outside. She called for her page.

A bell rang by her door and her page stepped inside. He stood in the middle of the room, with the audacity to stare directly at Augusta. She slapped him with the back of her hand. He shrunk back and looked down at the floor. He walked over to the bed and started to remove his clothes.

"No, not now," Augusta said.

The boy froze halfway out of his coat. Augusta showed him the locket.

"You will tell me what this is," she said.

"Mistress doesn't know?" he replied.

Augusta slapped him again. This time her nails left marks. His eyes watered.

"You will tell me what this is," she repeated.

He sniffled. "It's a watch."

"And a watch measures time," Augusta said to herself.

"It does," the boy affirmed.

"Tell me more," Augusta said.

She pulled the boy down on the bed next to her and put her arm around his shoulders. He pointed at the different parts of the watch, explaining their functions. The rods were called hands, and chased around the clockface in step with time. The clockface indicated where in time one was located. It made Augusta shudder violently. Time was an abhorrent thing, a human thing. It didn't belong here. It was that power which made flesh rot and dreams wither.

"Does it measure time?" Augusta said. "Or does it just move forward and call that time?"

The page blinked. "Time is time," he said.

"Time is time," Augusta echoed. "If it goes, it goes forward."

"That's what I was about to say," said the page.

"I know," Augusta replied. "This has happened before."

Augusta twisted the little knob on the side of the clock, and the longest hand started to move. A faint ticking sound filled the bower. The air trembled.

"This has happened before," Augusta said again.

She let go of the boy's shoulders, and he stood up. His shape was blurred somehow.

"I can't let you leave," Augusta said. "Not again."

"What do you mean, mistress?" said the boy.

"What are you called?" Augusta asked.

"Yarrow, mistress," the boy said.

Augusta blinked. "Not Thistle?"

"There is no Thistle here," Yarrow replied.

Augusta picked up a long knife that lay on her vanity. She grabbed Yarrow's jaw and quickly slit his throat. He gurgled as blood gushed down his shirt.

32

It wasn't a pit that they fell into, but a tunnel that twisted back and forth. Then, bright light. The impact came fast: rubble and gravel, sliding away under Dora's feet. She tumbled down a slope and came to a rest on her side, the satchel digging into her shoulder. Behind her, Albin yelled in terror on the way down. She grabbed his arm as he came by.

They sat halfway down an enormous mound of gravel. Below them stood the ruins of a town: heavy stone buildings with their roofs blown off and huge holes through which the overcast sky showed; here and there, the burnt skeletons of wooden houses. The streets were strewn with debris.

The company's house-carriage stood on its six wheels in a cleared square of street, walls unfolded to make a stage. As Albin and Dora crawled down the pile and came closer, Dora saw that the interior was decorated to look like a run-down room in the city: overturned chairs, a shattered mirror on the wall, a small dining table on which stood the remains of an abandoned meal. In the middle of the room, Nestor was dressed in a gray uniform adorned with silver. He was clean-shaven, a distinguished man approaching old age. Journeyman stood next to him, dressed in the same style. He was wearing a black helmet and held something that looked like a branch but must have been a weapon.

In front of them stood Director, in a torn dress and head-scarf. Her face was riddled with scars. She held her hands out in supplication.

"Have mercy, sir," she said in a broken alto. "There's nothing left of me. You promised to leave me alone, and yet you invaded my lands. You murdered my children. You burned my forests and razed my cities. Now everything is yours and nothing mine. Please leave us in peace. Let us live."

Nestor's voice boomed through the ruins. "You forced my hand!" He swept his hand to indicate the destruction. "Such a promising land it was, its people beautiful and pure. But you harbored a plague, and that plague must be cured."

"We have suffered enough," Director said.

"Then bow," said Nestor, "and give the rest of your children to me."

"Never," Director replied.

"This might work," Albin whispered to Dora where they sat in the rubble.

"What?" Dora asked, but Albin hushed her.

Onstage, Nestor smiled and pointed at Director. Journeyman lifted the black branch in his hands. A crack echoed through the city. Director slumped into a heap. Nestor turned outward.

"I am a just lord, with a just cause. My only wish is to better this world, to purify it of its ills. And so I have, once more." He stepped back into the shadows.

Journeyman stepped to the front of the stage and faltered. He drew a small square of paper from his breast pocket and looked at it. Then he said, "The Child of the Motherland is supposed to show up now and convince me to rise up against the General."

Director sat up and threw her hands out. "Well. We don't have an actor to do that."

Albin grabbed Dora's hand and squeezed it so hard it almost hurt.

"But if we end the play here, then . . ." Journeyman trailed off.

"Then it will be a tragedy and not a story of hope in the face of destruction," Director filled in. "Yes. But what's our alternative? Nestor can't play a child. We need an Apprentice."

Journeyman raised his hands and let them drop again. "All right," he said, and cleared his throat.

Albin's hand left Dora's, and before she could react she saw him careening down the slope.

Journeyman began: "Here ends the tale of—"

"No!" Albin shouted, halfway down the slope. "Wait!"

Journeyman and Director stared at him, incredulous.

Albin reached the ground and stumbled, skinning his knees. He got up so quickly that he almost fell over again, and ran to the stage. "I'll be your Apprentice! I'll do it," he panted. "I'll do it."

There was a long moment of silence.

"You," Director eventually said.

"Please," Albin said. "I can't stand to watch this."

As Albin and Director stared at each other, Dora made her way down, and Journeyman spotted her. He hopped down from the stage and ran over to wrap his arms around her. He smelled of himself and acrid dust and sweat. Dora raised a hand and put it on his back. She could feel his heart hammering at his ribs.

"You came back," he said.

Director clapped her hands. "No time to waste," she said. "Explanations later. We have to finish this play. Now. Journeyman, give the boy the manuscript."

Journeyman let go of Dora and held out the square of paper to Albin. Albin looked it over and nodded.

"I can do this."

"What are you doing out there?" Nestor said from the back of the stage. He walked outside, still in his uniform. He took a look at Dora and Albin, raised his eyebrows, and let out a short "Ah."

"I made an executive decision," Director said. "This is the Child of the Motherland."

"Very well," Nestor said. "Shall I do the last line again?"

"Please do," Director said, and lay down on the stage.

Journeyman climbed back up and held out a hand for Albin to join him.

Dora watched from the ground as Albin put on the role of the Child of the Motherland, effortlessly convincing the Soldier to rise up against the General. The Soldier shot the General, and confetti fell from the rafters as he cast his weapon down and held hands with the Child. By the time they were done, the entire troupe was crying. So was Albin. But they were smiling, too. Dora clapped her hands enthusiastically.

"Well," Nestor said when they were done. "We will need an explanation."

The troupe turned their heads toward Albin, who stood between Journeyman and Director.

"Apprentice died in a rockslide," Dora said from the ground. "I buried her on the mountain. That's all."

The troupe turned to Dora as one.

"How exactly did she die?" Nestor asked.

"She played her flute, and stones fell on her," Dora replied.

"Stupid girl," Director mumbled.

"We felt it, you see," Nestor said. "We just couldn't see what had happened. It never appeared in the playbook."

Director raised her eyes and gave Albin a stare that made him shrink back. "You lured her with you," Director said. "You must have convinced her. Made promises."

"That's not true, and you know it," Journeyman said. "Apprentice wanted to go ever since she came to us!" He pointed at Dora, then Albin. "And when these two showed up, of course she wanted to run off with them. She wanted to be with people who weren't us. Do you pay attention to anything that goes on here?"

Nestor and Director looked at each other.

"I don't . . ." Director said.

"She wanted to leave," Journeyman said. "She was bored. This wasn't the life she wanted."

"She should have said so."

"And get out how, exactly?" Journeyman retorted. "You know how often new actors show up."

Nestor sat down on the stage. He took his cap off and tossed it into the rubble. He rubbed at his chin, studying Albin.

"It's not our fault, and not theirs either," Journeyman said. "Apprentice wasn't cut out for this. She just didn't know it when she signed on."

Nestor cleared his throat. "Be that as it may, there is an empty spot that needs to be filled." He gave Albin and Dora a kindly smile. "You see, children, we can't put on our plays without an Apprentice. Everything goes wrong. The play you just saw? In the end, the Child of the Motherland comes to sow the Seed of Hope. Life would have sprung up again. That was one of Apprentice's tasks: hope. Without Apprentice, the world isn't saved. Yet we must keep putting on our plays. And little by little, the universe slides out of joint. Until now."

"I will stay," Albin said.

The others fell silent. Director, Nestor, and Journeyman stared at him. He looked each of them in the eyes.

"I will be Apprentice until you find a new one," he continued.

"You would?" Director said. "Why?"

Albin wiped at his face. It was still wet. "I found my parents. They're dead and gone. But this . . . I could do this. I saved a world. I want to do it again."

Nestor stroked his chin. "He does have the spark."

"But this is not a decision to be made lightly," Director said.

"I'm not making it lightly," Albin said.

"What about Dora?" Journeyman asked.

Dora looked at Albin, who gave her a stare. *I have a plan*, he had said. Dora had to trust him.

"I go where Albin goes," she said.

"Albin?" Director blinked. "Ah. Your name."

Nestor nodded. "Good name."

"That wouldn't be a problem, would it," Journeyman said, and moved to stand beside Dora. He looked up at her with a hopeful gleam in his eyes. "Them coming with us."

Nestor chuckled and shook his head. "It would certainly be a perk for some of us."

Director twirled the shawl between her fingers. "It's not a bad plan," she mused.

"So we are in agreement?" Nestor asked.

Director and Journeyman nodded.

"I see no reason to wait," Director said. "Nestor, will you do the honors?"

The troupe closed in around Dora and Albin. Journeyman embraced Dora and Albin from behind. Director slid her hand around Albin's shoulders. Nestor took Albin's face in his hands. Up close, Dora could see how the creases by Nestor's eyes were slightly paler than the rest of his face. The inside rims of his eyes were turning outward with age, but the irises were a clear and shifting brown, like leaves at the bottom of a winter puddle. He smelled of old teeth and face paint.

"What is your name?" he asked Albin.

"Albin Jönsson," Albin replied.

"Then say after me, 'I, Albin Jönsson, swear to serve as Apprentice until a new Apprentice is found.'"

Albin repeated Nestor's words. Nestor kissed his forehead. Then he took a step back.

"Welcome, my dears, to the Memory Theater," Director said. "We are going to put on an excellent show."

Albin slid into his role as Apprentice like hand into silken glove. He brought finesse and emotional presence to his characters. Director said he was a natural. They put on play after play, all fetched from Director's playbook. Dora watched and applauded.

There were things Albin could not do yet. Sometimes, the plays the company put on were about people who weren't human-shaped. There were stories about people with hive minds and spindly legs; stories about undulating beings that made Dora's eyes hurt; stories about people made of sound. Albin bravely put on costumes and imitated the others' movements and voices. Director said that he would eventually learn other forms, if he stayed.

In his spare time, Albin wrote. He wouldn't show anyone what it was; he had asked for paper and pen, and said it was a diary. Nestor had patted him on the shoulder and said it was therapeutic. Not even Dora was allowed to know.

This meant she had plenty of time to think. She dreamed about the mountains often: the great silence, the vast spaces, the calm of massive stone. She thought about seeing Grandmother and Grandfather again, about hearing the saajvoe sing.

Journeyman kept close, but not too close; he was waiting for something. Dora thought she knew what it was, but she didn't want to give it to him, and told him as much. Not ever? Journeyman had asked. Not ever, Dora had replied.

In the mountains, no one would look at her and hope for things. Dora found herself slowing down. Noise and movement became more stressful. She slept longer and longer. Albin said he worried about her. Nestor said that perhaps she was coming into her true nature, whatever that was. *What is the word for when you think of where you came from and become sad?* she asked Journeyman once. Homesick, he had answered. *You're homesick.*

One day, Albin came over to her as they were preparing for the sixteenth play, *The Great Tragedy of Ossa-Fara.* He was dressed in the dun robes of the Penitent Brother, face painted in a white mask.

"I need you to do something," he said.

"Yes," Dora said without hesitation.

"I said I had a plan," Albin continued. "It's time to make that plan happen."

He reached into the folds of his robe and drew out a bundle of papers. "Dora," he said, "I need you to put this in Director's book while we're putting on the play. They mustn't notice."

"Why?" Dora asked.

"Just trust me, please. Will you do this for me?"

"I will," Dora replied.

When all the actors were onstage and Director was holding a passionate speech as the great queen Ossa-Fara, stricken by madness and about to obliterate her own lands, Dora snuck behind the curtain and found Director's playbook where it lay on her dressing table. She lifted the cover, and it was empty. Dora stuck Albin's bundle of papers in there and went back to her couch in front of the stage.

The great queen Ossa-Fara was assassinated by the Penitent Brother, and the Crone sang her lilting song, and it was over.

"A middling performance," Nestor muttered as he took off the Crone's wig.

"You can't hit all the notes every single time," Journeyman said. "I thought it was great."

"Everyone!" Director shouted from behind the stage.

"What?" Nestor shouted back.

Director lifted the curtain and came out, brandishing the playbook. "There's a new play," she said.

"So soon?" Nestor said. "Must be urgent."

"It might be," Director said. "Just look at the title. I think we need to do it right away."

"What is it?" Albin asked.

"It seems to have your old enemy in it," Director said, and grinned.

33

The Fall of the Gardens

PROLOGUE

CHORUS:
  Welcome, one and all, into the Gardens,
  Where time does not exist, nor night or day,
  Where lords and ladies in eternal twilight
  Torture children, feast, and dance, and play.
  A lady, once cast out, returns to join them
  Unwittingly about to seal her fate.
  Here, we tell the tale of how Augusta
  Brought the Gardens to a tragic end.

SCENE I

A lawn, with small chairs and tables to the side. Two Revelers are playing croquet with a lump of meat. The Lady Mnemosyne watches from a divan. Augusta Prima enters from stage left.

AUGUSTA:

> Here I am at last, back from my travels;
> The road was long and bloody, full of murder,
> For I am a villain with a cause.
> Let me see if they have missed my presence.

Augusta takes another step, revealing herself.

AUGUSTA:

> I have returned, beloved gentlefolk!
> Once cast out, I hope now to be welcomed back.

MNEMOSYNE:

> Augusta! I know not of what you speak.
> Please take a club and play croquet with us.

REVELER 1:

> Yes, Augusta, play a game with us!

REVELER 2:

> There is wine and all the birds are singing.

REVELER 1:

> We killed a servant and devour'd him.
> His kidney makes a perfect croquet ball.

The Revelers take Augusta's hands. They dance across the stage. Augusta laughs and dances along.

REVELERS:

> Sing for youth and beauty, sing for evermore!
> Sing for feast and revelry, sing for nature's gifts!

AUGUSTA:

> I think I was elsewhere but have forgotten.
> How beautiful this never-ending feast.

Augusta continues to sing and dance, but from her hands, a miasma begins to ooze like black smoke. She walks across the stage, caressing trees, flowers, and the Revelers. The trees droop, the flowers wilt, and the Revelers' clothes begin to fray where she has touched them. Augusta dances past Mnemosyne and lightly touches her hand.

Reveler 1 stops and clutches his chest.

REVELER 1:

> Zounds! What is this stinging feeling?
> 'Tis like an arrow in my shriveled heart.

REVELER 2:

> I, too, can feel a dreadful shiver inside.
> Something is afoot; I sense it coming.

AUGUSTA:

> Whatever do you mean, my lovely darlings?

Reveler 1 shudders and slumps to the ground. Reveler 2 coughs up a stream of blood. Mnemosyne holds up her hands and looks at them. As she does so, her gown falls from her shoulders to reveal a skeletal rib cage.

MNEMOSYNE:

> What is this awful thing? Is Death a-coming?
> We have not invited it to visit.

Reveler 2 sinks to his knees. Mnemosyne stands up and points at Augusta.

MNEMOSYNE:

Augusta, why does your touch bring a rot?

AUGUSTA:

I know not what you mean; I'm merely dancing.
Never would I put my kind in danger.

MNEMOSYNE:

Doom has come to visit and you brought it.
A curse on you, oh foul Lady Augusta!

Mnemosyne falls to the ground and lets out one last breath. Augusta tears at her own shirt; beneath, her flesh is falling apart.

AUGUSTA:

It cannot be! The Gardens are immortal!
What have we done to see this awful fate?
My lady and my fellows are succumbing
To some strange plague, and so am I.
What have I done? What will become of me?
How sad, to end like this, a ruin,
Where once I was a lady of the court.

Vines climb up Augusta's arms and cover her face. She slumps to the ground and lies still.

CHORUS:

Here ends the tale of foul Augusta Prima,
A murderer, a kidnapper, and thief.

The lords and ladies were all punished justly,
The Gardens' magic broken and dismissed.
The children are now free to return home
To mortal lands where they might live in peace.
Ne'er again will foul Augusta roam;
Good has triumphed, and the world is whole.

THE END

34

Augusta stood on the grass, reeling. On the dais before her, Mnemosyne's corpse was sinking into the throne, which had sprouted vines and crushed her in its embrace. Walpurgis lay in front of her, one hand around Mnemosyne's foot. His face had collapsed in on itself; tiny shoots stretched into the air from the top of his head. Cymbeline and Virgilia embraced each other in a heap in the middle of the lawn. And there was Euterpe, naked in the rhododendron, overtaken by growth; ferns shot up like spears through her chest, unfurling in the sunlight. Everything was quiet save for the rustle of growing things. The air smelled of dew and grass and rot. It was dawn.

The servants still stood here and there on the lawn. Augusta saw now how emaciated they were, how their dresses and livery hung moldy and moth-eaten on their thin frames. They were all staring at her.

Augusta looked down at herself. Nothing had happened to

her. She was as she had been before: the borrowed breeches and coat, her body within. She alone was untouched. She kneeled by Euterpe's body and shook it gently.

"Sister," she said. "Wake up."

Euterpe fell apart like a rotten log. The inside teemed with life: beetles, maggots, sprouting seeds.

Augusta's cheeks felt hot and wet. It was hard to breathe.

"Remarkable," a voice said.

Augusta turned around. Ghorbi.

"You," Augusta said. "Did you do this?"

"Of course not," Ghorbi replied. "I merely watched."

"But all this." Augusta gestured at the mayhem. "It's you. It must be you."

"I think not," Ghorbi said. "But I have my suspicions. It looked a lot like a play. You were talking in blank verse."

"I'm not dead."

"No, you're not." Ghorbi paused. "You probably should be. But you're not."

Augusta shook her head. "I don't understand."

"Let's be clear," Ghorbi said. "You had this coming. Albin survived, did you know? I'm sure he had plans for you."

"Albin," Augusta said. "Albin."

A boy, a page. Insolent. She had killed him. He and Ghorbi must have conspired. She looked at what was left of poor Euterpe, who had only just now danced across the lawn.

"This is all your fault," Augusta growled. "Yours and Albin's."

She threw herself at Ghorbi, who slid out of her way.

"I see you haven't learned a thing," Ghorbi said.

Augusta punched at her, but her fist met empty air. She cried out in frustration, and Ghorbi chuckled.

"You'll see," Augusta said. "I'll be like you. I'll travel the worlds. I'll be a celebrated guest in every court. And I'll have my vengeance."

Ghorbi's expression grew serious.

"Not like me," Ghorbi said. "Never like me. You don't know how to be a guest. You only know how to intrude, to subjugate. You wouldn't be a guest; you'd be a terrifying invader. In any case . . ." Ghorbi looked over Augusta's shoulder. "You'd best hurry."

Footsteps came through the grass. Augusta turned her head and saw a half-circle of servants closing in on her. Her chest seized with something like fear.

"Help me," she begged Ghorbi. "For friendship's sake."

Ghorbi shook her head. "You are no one's friend, Augusta." She took a few steps back.

The servants surrounded Augusta now. They were not at all the cowed children that had once attended the courtiers.

Augusta pointed at the biggest one, a sturdy-looking youth.

"You," she said, in her lady voice. "Pack me a bag for traveling."

The servant stared at her, right in the eyes. Then he charged.

Augusta turned around and ran into the forest. Twigs tore at her as she pushed her way through underbrush. Her lungs hurt. Behind her, the ululating cries of the hunt.

35

The house-carriage sat in the middle of a lawn that had burst into wild growth. In front of it stood a pavilion with the over-grown remains of a divan. Here and there, bone gleamed in wet grass. The sun shone down; clouds were scudding away over the treetops.

"Here we are," Director said, "frontstage and all, for once."

"Thank you," Albin said.

"I can't see her anywhere," Albin said. He was pacing the lawn, still wearing Reveler One's ruined coat. Nearby, Journeyman stepped out of Mnemosyne's dress and folded it.

Director took her wig off. "Augusta should have perished here with the rest of the Gardens," she said.

"She's not here!" Albin replied.

He pointed at the green-clad corpse on the throne, still crowned in laurel. "That's Mnemosyne. And that's Euterpe over there, and Walpurgis, and Virgilia . . . but I don't see Augusta. Where is she?" His voice rose to a shout.

"Walpurgis," Dora said.

She picked her way across the lawn to the corpse whose garb was being overrun by tiny flowers. Walpurgis was almost reduced to bones, but the ringlets of his hair were still perfect. Dora bent down and touched them. They came loose from the skull and fell into her hands. It occurred to her that maybe she should grieve for him. But all she felt was tired. Walpurgis had not deserved to be a father.

"Goodbye," she said to Walpurgis where he lay.

"Why isn't she here?" Albin said again. "She's supposed to be! That was the whole idea!"

"What idea, Albin?" Director said in a low voice.

Dora straightened. "Albin wrote the play."

"You did what?" Nestor said incredulously.

Albin shot Dora an angry glance. "You promised you wouldn't tell."

"But you just did," Dora replied.

"I want to hear it from you, Albin," Director said slowly, and walked over to where he stood.

Albin swallowed. "I wrote the play. I wrote the play and made Dora put it in your book."

Nestor rubbed his chin, smearing his Reveler Two makeup. His eyes were hard. "I take it you didn't join us for the reasons you gave."

"I didn't lie," Albin replied. "Everything I said was true. I have nowhere to go. And I love being an actor."

"You lied by omission," Nestor stated.

Journeyman looked at Dora helplessly. "Were you in on this?"

"I promised not to tell," Dora said.

Director had made it all the way over to Albin now and was staring down at him. Her voice was cold. "Albin," she said.

Albin looked up at her, hands balled into fists.

"Do you understand what you have done?" Director continued. "Do you understand what it means to write something that did not happen?"

"We are not gods," Nestor said. "We are a function. We are memory. And memory is not a power to be abused."

"You used us," Journeyman said, still looking at Dora. "You used us to alter the fabric of the multiverse."

"This place is evil!" Albin shouted into Director's face. "Everything about it is evil! Augusta is a murderer! I did the right thing! And now she isn't here!" His voice broke. "She isn't here."

Director's expression softened. "I think it's time you let this go, Albin. Move on with your life. Or this will eat you alive."

Albin covered his eyes. Dora could see his lips trembling. She walked over to comfort him, but he turned away. She heard him cry with small noises. It made her chest hurt.

"That was the show of a lifetime," said a voice.

Ghorbi stood at the edge of the lawn, wrapped in her shadowy robes. The sunlight didn't seem to touch her.

Nestor's expression turned sour. "You were watching all along?"

"I was," Ghorbi said. "Hello again, keeper of plays."

"So that's Ghorbi," Journeyman said. "I've always wondered."

Director smiled. "That's her indeed."

"Did you come here to congratulate yourself on a game well played?" Nestor said.

Ghorbi looked down at him. "I don't play games. I just know when I can help and when I can't. Thank you for returning the favor."

Nestor sneered. "I'll bet you were waiting for something really big. These children have had us running back and forth across all the worlds."

Ghorbi gave him a sad smile. "I did you a favor, a long time ago. I called it in. That is the way of things. You want something that I cannot give. That is why you are angry."

Unexpectedly, Nestor's eyes filled with tears. "I just wish you would have loved me back," he said in a small voice.

"I know," Ghorbi said. "But I didn't."

She turned to the others. "I have business to attend to. I just didn't want to miss the climax." She raised an eyebrow at Dora. "I have not forgotten our deal. But your life will be long, and I'm not in a hurry. Be well."

"Wait," Albin said. "What became of Augusta?"

"Last I saw, your fellow servants were hunting her," Ghorbi said. "A beautiful case of poetic justice."

"So she is dead."

"I can't say," Ghorbi replied. "But I have trouble believing she could outrun that sort of fury."

Albin looked at his feet.

"Can you be content with that?" Ghorbi asked.

He looked up, and his eyes were hollow. "I'm tired."

Ghorbi nodded. "Perhaps it is time to begin your own life."

Then she was gone.

The carriage swayed as it traveled along a stream between worlds. Muted light flickered through the stained-glass windows and danced over the company's faces. Nestor and Director were staring at the map, speaking in low voices. Director had her playbook out and was pointing to it and then to the map. Journeyman was fussing with pots and pans in the kitchen. Whatever he was making smelled of spices. Albin sat in one of the armchairs, feet dangling over an armrest. Dora sat on the floor next to him. Albin reached down to stroke Dora's hair.

"It's grown back," he said.

"It has," Dora agreed. "Are you still sad?"

"I am," Albin replied. "And angry. And heartsick."

"Will you always be?"

Albin scratched her scalp a little. "I don't think so. But I have to be for a while. You can't fix it. Just let me be like that."

Dora patted his hand. "I will."

Director and Nestor came over. Director sat down in the chair across from Albin, and Nestor stood next to her with a hand on the backrest. Behind them, Journeyman looked up from the stove.

"We need to talk," Director said, and her face was set.

Albin's hand left Dora's head, and he sat up straight.

Director pointed at Albin. "You did something very stupid," she said. "You abused our power."

"What are you going to do?" Albin asked in a small voice. "Are you going to punish me?"

Director shook her head. "No."

"What you did was idiotic," Nestor said. "But you have a talent for drama."

"We would like to offer you a permanent position," Director continued. "You won't be writing any more plays, though."

"I'm going to die soon," Nestor said conversationally. "Then Director will become Grande Dame, and Journeyman will be

Director, and you will be Journeyman. And someone else will be Apprentice."

"You will make a wonderful Director eventually," Director said. "I know it."

Albin sat very still in his chair.

Director rose. "We'll let you mull it over."

She and Nestor returned to the map. Journeyman turned his attention back to the cooking pot.

"I don't know what to do," Albin said.

"I do," Dora replied. "You should stay here. This is a good place for you."

"What do you mean, 'You should stay'?"

Dora shifted so she could look straight at Albin. *What is the word for when you think of where you came from and become sad? Homesick.*

"I have followed you all this time," Dora said, "when you were looking for your name and then looking for Augusta. You protected me in the Gardens, so I protected you outside. But now you're safe. You're grown up. You don't need my protection anymore. And so it's my turn. I want to go home."

Albin looked at her, and his eyes glittered. "I know you have to go."

Dora rose up on her knees and cradled his face in her hands. He was almost a man now, but she could feel his delicate jaw under the beard.

"You can come visit me on the mountain," she said. "You know where it is."

"But not frontstage," Albin replied. "I'll always be backstage. Watching you."

"Maybe they'll make an exception."

Albin shrugged helplessly. "Maybe."

Dora put her arms around him.

"I can hear your heart," he mumbled into her chest. "It's so slow."

"Tell me a story," Dora said.

Acknowledgments

This book took a very long time to write, and I did not walk the road alone.

I would like to thank my parents, Kerstin Leijd-Tidbeck and Göran Tidbeck, who have always lent me their unconditional support. I would also like to thank loved ones, friends, and colleagues who have helped me, inspired me, and given invaluable advice: Patrik Åkervinda, Robin Steen, Anna Eriksson, Elin Gustafsson, Anna-Karin Linder, Fredrik von Post, the Moira crew, Haralambi Markov, Lisa Wool-Rim Sjöblom, Pablo Valcárcel, Rochita Loenen-Ruiz, Leah Thomas, Nahal Ghanbari, Karin Waller, Nene Ormes, the Word Murderers, Christine "Sonya" Malapetsa, Jay Wolf, Sara Bergmark Elfgren, Amal El-Mohtar, Niclas Hell, and Kjell Hedgard Hugaas.

Thank you to my agent, Reneé Zuckerbrot, who believed in this story and guided me every step of the way.

Last, a thank-you to my editor, Tim O'Connell, at Penguin Random House for his keen eye, patience, and dedication; and to Anna Kaufman and Robert Shapiro.

Karin Tidbeck is originally from Stockholm, Sweden. She lives and works in Malmö as a freelance writer, translator, and creative writing teacher, and writes fiction in Swedish and English. She debuted in 2010 with the Swedish short story collection Vem är Arvid Pekon? Her English debut, the 2012 collection Jagannath, received the 2013 Crawford Award and was shortlisted for the World Fantasy Award. She is the author of the novel Amatka.

A NOTE ON THE TYPE

The text of this book was set in Seria, a typeface designed by the Dutch designer Martin Majoor (b. 1960) for the FontFont foundry in 2000. Seria was drawn to have long ascenders and descenders and very fine detailing. The Seria family of fonts contains both a serif and a sans serif alphabet.

Typeset by Scribe, Philadelphia, Pennsylvania
Printed and bound by Friesens, Altona, Manitoba
Designed by Anna B. Knighton